To Arthur

Clovenhoof &
The Trump of
Doom

by Heide Goody and Iain Grant

Pigeon Park Press

1

Paperback ISBN: 978-0-9933655-7-7

Published by Pigeon Park Press

www.pigeonparkpress.com

Cover artwork by Mike Watts – www.bigbeano.co.uk

"You know, it doesn't really matter what they write as long as you've got a young and beautiful piece of ass."
Donald Trump

31st October 2016

Sutton Coldfield, Birmingham

It was the Toblerone which finally convinced Clovenhoof and Michael the world was about to end.

It had, all in all, been a successful Halloween for Jeremy Clovenhoof. For his first couple of years on Earth, he had sulked on Halloween. What was the point of trying to dress up and scare people when the good folk of England (who were either too blind to notice or too polite to comment) didn't realise that Satan himself lived among them? Then he had hit upon the marvellous idea of going out Trick or Treating as himself. Some papier-mâché horns on top of his actual horns, a pair of hairy red socks to cover his goaty legs, and a ton of red make-up over his already red face and people were all "Ooh, isn't he scary?" and "Oh, Mr Clovenhoof, you look like the very devil himself," to which he would then reply, in the spirit of the season, "Damn right I bloody do, now give me all your sweets, biatch!"

This year, Clovenhoof had tried a different Halloween tactic and gone Trick or Treating at a wholesaler's warehouse. He had knocked and demanded sweet goods and the security guard had obliged readily. Clovenhoof reflected afterwards that his tone of voice and use of a plastic but nonetheless realistic Desert Eagle water pistol might have given the security guard the wrong idea; but if the stupid old duffer thought he was being robbed rather than playfully entreated by a fun-loving local, that was his fault.

By ten that night, Clovenhoof sat in his squalid flat, surrounded by the chocolates, sweets, seven mobile phones and two fridge freezers he had gained that evening. He sat, a refreshing glass of Lambrini at his side, and cracked open a giant tube of Toblerone chocolate. He stared in horror.

The triangular blocks of chocolate had changed. The mountain-valley-mountain-valley pattern remained but – by Satan's balls! – there was a lot more valley and a lot less mountain than he was expecting.

"Damn you, you cuckoo-clock inventing, Nazi-gold hoarding chocolate-deniers!" he shouted. "This demands a strongly worded letter. Or a turd in a box."

Clovenhoof decided sending the Swiss chocolatiers a turd in a box would be by far the clearer message. He was all ready to make a start on it, when he paused. At first he wasn't sure why. Something niggled at him. Something almost forgotten but deeply important. He trotted to the sofa, dug into its dark, dusty and occasionally squidgy crevices and came up with a crumpled and browning piece of paper. He scoured the four by four grid, and the phrases written in a florid and ancient hand.

"*The mountain of sweetmeats will be separated from its brothers,*" he read. "That's it. Oh, by my sweet swinging dong, that's it!"

There was a sharp knock at the door. It was Michael. The Archangel Michael. They had been neighbours twice in their lives (if life was even the right word for immortal beings): once when they had stood shoulder to shoulder among the glorious Host of Heaven and a second time when Michael had been exiled to Earth and forced to live in the flat downstairs. He now lived a short distance across town with the small but perfectly formed Andy and never visited Clovenhoof if he could avoid it.

Michael was currently out of breath and waving a piece of yellowed paper identical to the one Clovenhoof held. "*The mountain of sweetmeats will be separated from its brothers,*" he panted.

"I know!" said Clovenhoof.

"That's fifteen of them!"

"I know!" shouted Clovenhoof.

"This is all your doing, isn't it?" said the fallen but immaculately tailored angel.

"Me?" retorted Clovenhoof. "This has your sticky fingerprints all over it!"

"Are you suggesting...?"

"No, I'm bloody accusing!"

"Would you both shut up!" yelled Nerys, coming down the stairs from the second floor.

Nerys Thomas, man enthusiast and upstairs neighbour, was one of the only two on Earth who knew exactly what these otherworldly blokes were. She presently bore an expression, if not like thunder, certainly resembled rumbling black clouds gathered over the hills of her Welsh homeland.

"It's gone ten o'clock. I've got work tomorrow. And I've had to let Ben stay in my flat tonight because some pillock told him *The Human Centipede* was a nature documentary and he's too traumatised to sleep. What's going on?"

"Nostradamus' Apocalypse Bingo," said Clovenhoof.

"The end of the world," said Michael.

"Oh, good," said Nerys. "And here was me thinking it was something important. And real."

"No, it is," insisted Clovenhoof. He waggled his bit of paper in front of her face.

Nerys held it still while she read. "*All The Countries of the World will end in flame and ordeal in the year when each of the sixteen signs comes to pass.*"

"Exactly," said Clovenhoof. "Laughing boy here is no doubt behind it. When the world ends, he goes home to the Celestial City. Boom."

"That's very cynical, Jeremy," said Michael. "You, on the other hand, are well-known for wanting God's creation undone. It's your *raison d'etre*."

"I haven't raisoned anything, chum. Besides, I haven't seen the latest series of *Game of Thrones*, and I've heard rumours they're going to bring *Topless Darts on Ice* back. I've got too much to live for."

"Right. Let me make this clear." Nerys steered the two of them back into Clovenhoof's flat. "The world is not going to end. There's no such thing as Nostradamus' Apocalypse Lottery."

"Bingo," corrected Michael.

"Bingo, then. It's stupid. Who came up with it anyway?"

Clovenhoof flicked her forehead. "Nostradamus, putty brain."

"Never heard of it," she said. "And if you touch me again, I'll rip your horns off. All three of them."

"I like her," smiled Michael. "But the signs are all there, Nerys. Look." He pointed at one of the squares. *"In the River of January, the divers' pool will be as emerald."*

"And?" she said.

"The Rio Olympics. The swimming pool turned green. No one knew why."

"And this," indicated Clovenhoof.

"The storehouse of the Britons' homes will be no more," she read.

"And BHS has just closed all its shops."

"The thin white duke and Major Thomas will die as one," said Michael.

"The motored head will sing of the ace of spades no more," said Clovenhoof.

"The forest ape of Cincinnatus will die with child in arms."

"Europe's crown of stars will be broken by England's decree."

"What?" said Nerys. "Brexit is going cause the end of the world? I mean, it has kind of scuppered my plans for a cheap Spanish holiday next year, but it can't bring about the end of the world. Can it?"

Michael and Clovenhoof looked at each other.

"There's only one prediction left to come true," spoke Michael.

"And what's that?" asked Nerys, scouring Clovenhoof's parchment. He had crossed off each of the predictions and drawn naked women in the borders.

"The Trump of Doom will sound in victory, one week after All Hallows' Day," supplied Clovenhoof.

"Trump?" she said.

"Obviously—" said Michael, in the tones of one who believed it was obvious to no one but himself, "—we would normally take the Trump of Doom to refer to the final trumpet blast announcing the Day of Judgement and the arrival of the Almighty's Kingdom. But in this case—"

"Trump," said Clovenhoof. "Eighth of October."

"The US election," added Michael.

"Oh, crap," said Nerys. "I don't want the world to end."

"Nor I," agreed Michael.

"Not till I see all of *Game of Thrones*," said Clovenhoof.

Nerys gave a sudden, shrill and slightly hysterical laugh. "But Trump can't win. That's ridiculous. He's a buffoon."

"We can pray he doesn't," said Michael. "But that's down to the will of the American people."

"We have to stop him," said Clovenhoof. "We have to make him lose."

"That would be grossly underhanded and undemocratic," said Michael.

"You don't have to sell it," said Clovenhoof. "You had me at underhanded. What's the alternative?"

Michael pouted his perfect lips in thought. "We could undo one of the other predictions."

"Bring Lemmy back to life?" said a hopeful Nerys.

"Travel back in time and dye the Olympic pools blue?" said Clovenhoof.

The archangel looked pensive. "I will think of something."

"Jolly good," said Clovenhoof. He gave Michael an uncharacteristic shrug. "Well, you plough your furrow and I'll plough mine and we'll see who saves the world first, eh?"

"Well, indeed," said Michael. "I will see you both later." He paused. "In this world or the next, eh?"

When Michael had left, Nerys said: "Just one question,"

"Yes?"

"Why are there two new fridge freezers in your flat?"

"Trick or Treating, my shapely friend," Clovenhoof grinned. He flicked his fingers and Michael's credit card, deftly pinched moments before, appeared between his fingertips. "It is the season of surprises after all."

1st *November 2016*

The next morning found Michael pacing the rug, knowing that he'd hate himself later for flattening the pile. His small but perfectly formed boyfriend Andy brought him a cup of tea and some toast.

"You'll flatten the pile."

"I know."

"What's bothering you, babe?"

"Everything," said Michael. "Ebola outbreaks. Brexit. Syria. The changes to Toblerone."

"Yes, 2016 has been a git of a year. Although," Andy gently pointed out, "some of those are obviously worse than others."

"But I can't stand by and let these things happen."

Andy patted the sofa beside him. "You know, there are some things we just can't fix, Michael."

"No, that can't be true. We must be able to undo at least one of them. Maybe Brexit."

"Well, unless Bobby Ewing wakes up in the shower and discovers Nigel Farage was just a dream, I don't see how."

"I can't just sit by and watch Europe distance itself from us as if we're an embarrassing auntie that's turned up drunk to a party," said Michael.

"The Brexit vote was a shock, but there's nothing you or I can do to reverse it."

"But you love Europe, don't you? Think of the wine, the cheese, the colourful trousers."

"You know I love all of those things, Michael, but we can get trousers from Gap if needs be."

"Oh, *Gap*! That's your answer to everything. That and Pilates. And sex."

"You're working yourself up."

Michael shook his head. "Andy, I need to do something *practical* to bring Europe together. The Prime Minister says she will press the button on Article 50 and start the Brexit process; but she's not pressed it yet. I know I can make a difference. I can do something to reunite all Europeans. It's been done before, after all."

"Nice idea," nodded Andy. "Maybe you could copy that."

Michael stood in thought for a moment. "No," he sighed. "I don't think a war with Germany is the way to go." He walked over to the window and looked out at the quiet side street. Boldmere was special of course; this leafy suburb of Birmingham, one of Britain's less glamorous cities, was *home*. "What unites the people of Boldmere with the people of France, Spain and Estonia? What inspires their hopes and dreams?"

"The European Space Agency?" suggested Andy.

"Not really going so well at the moment," mused Michael. "Losing that Mars probe isn't the sort of upbeat vibe we're looking for."

There was a stirring from the corner. Michael glanced at the sleeping bag where their rumpled house guest Heinz Takala raised his head. Heinz – Finn, photographer, artist, occasional Dadaist philosopher and naked bon viveur – had been staying with them for nearly a week. His latest exhibition had caused quite a stir in Birmingham's art scene. Critics suggested seeing a Finnish perspective on the life of ordinary Brummies was refreshingly disruptive; the tabloids said getting hundreds of people to take their clothes off in public for a photograph was the real reason for all of the attention. The Sutton Coldfield Recorder had perhaps captured it the best with the headline: *Scandinavian Perv turns Brummies into Bummies*. The exhibition launch party had been held in a Digbeth warehouse at the weekend, and Heinz had been sleeping in their lounge since then. There was a pile of promotional bottom-themed nutcrackers in the hall they'd be having words about fairly soon.

"You should look at Eurovision my friend," said Heinz, sitting up, his pale chest contrasting with the Osbourne & Little wallpaper. (In Michael's view, a houseguest overstaying his welcome was only marginally worse that a houseguest who didn't make the effort to colour co-ordinate themselves with the décor).

"Eurovision?" said Andy sceptically.

"Nothing brings Europeans together like it."

"Does it, though?" said Andy. "The assassination of an Austro-Hungarian archduke also brought Europeans together, but I wouldn't recommend it."

Heinz rubbed the sleep from his eyes. "You know of course that I performed for my country, yes?"

"You were in a Eurovision act?" Michael said.

"Of course. I do not joke about such things. Do you remember the Finnish entry for eighty two?" His face was alight with hope.

His hosts both confessed that they did not.

"Ah well. Like so many great things we were sadly overlooked. Our band was Kojo and we had the most amazing song. It challenged everyone's beliefs. If I am honest that is probably why we scored no points at all. Too challenging."

"How was it challenging?" asked Andy.

"It was called *Nuku Pommiin*, which means "Sleep to the bomb". Its central message was the best way to overcome a nuclear war would be to sleep through it. Deep, huh?"

"Deep, yes, of course," said Michael charitably. "Did you really not get a single point?"

"*Nil point*. It's an achievement of sorts, not everyone could do that. I had the most important job of hitting the big drum. Powerful message, you see. It needed that dramatic percussion."

Michael was thoughtful. "A song is a great way to get a message across." He went to his laptop and his fingers flew across the keyboard as his thoughts ordered themselves. He checked the details against the calendar on his computer. "Astonishing. The last day for registrations is today."

"Registration?" said Andy.

"To enter next year's Eurovision song contest. I think I will take that as a sign that this is what I need to do."

"To—? I'm sorry, I'm confused. How is entering the Eurovision contest going to fix what has been a shitty year?"

"Because we will reinvigorate and reunite a fragmented Europe, remind those Brexiteers what they are throwing away, and stop Article 50 in its tracks."

Andy kissed the top of Michael's head. "Well some of us have to go to work. If you're flying out to fix things today, send me a postcard, yeah? Mind you, Eurovision isn't until late spring, so I guess it's safe to get two chops out of the freezer?" He glanced across at Heinz. "Or is it three? I'll leave it with you, babe."

Michael nodded absently as he filled out the registration form. "Done! Now all I need is a song and a band. Where should we start, Heinz?"

Heinz massaged his neck thoughtfully. "I know the answer to this. My gorgeous Liam. I've mentioned him I think?"

"Once or twice, yes. Quite graphically."

"Liam and I are on a break at the moment, but we'll be drawn back to each other's arms before long. It is the magnetism, you know? It is raw, animal and so very ... rude." Heinz sighed and gazed wistfully into the middle distance. Discreetly, Michael coughed to bring him back. "Yes. Anyway, you would *never* guess who Liam's aunt is."

"No, you're right," said Michael. "Why don't you tell me?"

"Liam's aunt is Aisling McQuillan. Isn't that amazing?"

"And who is that?"

Heinz tapped the side of his nose and gave a playful smile. "I am about to let you into one of the biggest secrets of Eurovision. You know how Ireland won Eurovision three times, back in the day, yes? Well, all three songs were written by Aisling McQuillan. It won't say that if you go and look them up of course, but secretly they were. She is Ireland's secret weapon."

"Secret weapon, eh?"

Two hours later, Michael's stylish glass whiteboard was covered. Heinz had drawn a free-form mind map that looked like an explosion in a lollipop factory and Michael had created an orderly list. Michael reviewed his task list.

1 - *Find and recruit Aisling McQuillan to write song*
2 - *Assemble band*
3 - *Take act to Geneva and persuade European Broadcasting Network to bring Eurovision forward.*
4 - *Unite Europe through the power of song.*
5 - *Stop the end of the world.*

It was a good plan. It was a simple plan. What could go wrong?

Heinz wrapped up the phone call he was making. "Hey, good news," he told Michael. "I found Aisling. We can go and meet her."

"Where in Ireland does she live?"

"She doesn't. There was a terrible confusion with royalties, tax and money laundering. You know how it is. Anyway, she can't go back there. She's running a goat farm near Athens."

"Athens?"

"In Greece."

"I know where it is." Michael gave it some thought. "Well, that could work well for finding one of our other recruits."

"Who are the other recruits?" asked Heinz.

"I have created an algorithm—"

"You are a slave to the rhythms, Michael."

"An *algorithm* based on the personal characteristics of past European winners," said Michael. "I found twenty five markers for Eurovision success, which I can cross-reference against certain sources I am able to access for the population of Europe."

"Sources. Sounds not entirely legal," beamed Heinz.

"If GCHQ and the French DGSI insist on having such weak cyber-security then they can only expect benign operatives such as myself to make good use of their data."

"You are so naughty. I love it. What sort of markers did you find?"

"Ownership of a car with silver paintwork is one," said Michael. "As is a history of phoning in to local radio shows. One of the strongest markers, however, is where people have been arrested for disturbing the peace by performing music."

Heinz gave Michael a grave look. "I hope you are not mixing up cause and effect, Michael. It's a question of whether that was before or *after* their Eurovision success. There's many a Eurovision musician who's been misunderstood when they tried to recreate their glory days for an ungrateful public. I should know this."

Michael pushed aside that entirely reasonable point. The research was done now, and he would stick by it. "The statistics are reliable. The first person we need to look up is in Bulgaria. We can go there when we've met Aisling."

"Perfect. We just have a small shopping list. Aisling lives a very simple life on her goat farm, so we should take her these small luxuries."

Somewhere over the Atlantic

"Can I ask you a question, Grace?" Clovenhoof said to his neighbour in seat 27F.

Clovenhoof's flight to the US on his Trump-stopping mission had been a perfectly entertaining one so far. He had ordered a paleo-kosher-halal meal at check-in and spent much of the early flight wondering what a Jewish-Muslim-caveman would be given to eat (carrots and grapes, it turned out). Afterwards, he ordered a vast quantity of spirit and liqueur miniatures from the drinks trolley and turned his drop-down tray into a combined tiny cocktail bar and equally tiny bowling alley, using a left over grape as a ball. Then he discovered the delights of the in-flight shop, which provided him with several hours of entertainment until the stewardess told him buying toy aeroplanes, snapping the wings off and giving them to random passengers with what she described as a "Seriously deranged look in your eyes, sir" was not on.

"Sure, Jeremy," said Grace. She had been a delightful fellow traveller on the transatlantic flight: enjoying miniature bottle bowling, and the gift of a wingless toy plane in the spirit it was intended.

"Who is this Donald Trump guy?" asked Clovenhoof.

Grace was thoughtful for a moment. "Mrs Karnacki says he's a spoilt little rich kid who never grew up. I know he's very rich. He owns a lot of buildings and he's built a lot more. And he was on that TV show where the people have to fight it out for the top job in his company. And now he wants to be President."

"Okay," said Clovenhoof, making notes on the back of a gin and grape stained napkin. "He wins the throne—"

"Election."

"Right. He wins the election by fighting it out with the other claimants."

"Hillary Clinton."

"And that's a ... girl?"

"Sure," said Grace, taking one of Clovenhoof's remaining grapes and popping it in her mouth.

"And they fight with … what?" asked Clovenhoof, hoping the answer was "Damn big swords" or, even better, "Kangaroos and hand grenades".

"The electoral college system," said Grace.

"Okay," said Clovenhoof, who didn't know what an electoral college system was and feared that big swords, kangaroos and hand grenades wouldn't play a part. "Explain."

And so Grace explained while Clovenhoof ordered several packs of peanuts and drew various tortured faces on the individual nuts with his complimentary airline pen. There were phrases in Grace's explanation like "indirect election", "apportionment", "Congressional district method" and "Twelfth Amendment." Clovenhoof, despite appearances, was a quick learner and soon grasped the intricacies of the electoral system governing one of the largest democracies in the world.

"That's bonkers," he said.

"Bonkers?" said Grace.

"Mad. Crazy. Cuckoo," said Clovenhoof. "So, a candidate could win more of the individual people's votes and still not become President?"

"True," said Grace.

"And if you were somewhere like – Wyoming, was it? – your vote is actually worth over three times as much as somewhere like New York."

"I guess so. I might have to check with Mrs Karnacki about that."

"*And* even if you and everyone in your state decided to vote for the elephant candidate—"

"The Republican."

"—the electors you voted for could, if they wanted to, all give their own votes to other side."

"Sure. But that would be naughty."

"Oh, well, long as everyone knows it's naughty." Clovenhoof rolled his eyes. "So, big question, Grace: will this Trump geezer win?"

"No," said Grace firmly.

"All right," said Clovenhoof, very happy to hear that his world-saving mission might turn into a Stateside holiday at Michael's expense. "Why not?"

"Because he is a racist and a sexist who says dumb and hurtful things."

"I say dumb and hurtful things all the time," said Clovenhoof.

"Are you trying to become President of the United States?"

"No."

"He hates woman. He hates Mexicans. He hates African-Americans. That's already over half the people who can vote. There's no way he can win."

Clovenhoof chuckled. "So, I take it you'll be voting for this Hillary character, then?"

"I can't," said Grace.

"Why not?" said Clovenhoof.

"I'm only nine, Jeremy."

For the remainder of the flight, while Grace watched movies and her parents snored beneath their eye masks, Clovenhoof completed two important jobs. The first was putting each of the horror-faced peanuts in its individual miniature spirits bottle prison, telling them in turn what their crime was, and why they shouldn't be such a cry-baby about their just and eternal punishment. The second was finalising his plan of action. He had Donald J. Trump's itinerary downloaded on his phone and a near limitless pot of cash in the form of Michael's credit card. American was his oyster and Trump, it seemed, was the speck of dirt that he had to stop becoming its pearl.

As the plane touched down at Miami International Airport – with no wings snapping, no wheels flying off and no opportunity to use the big yellow emergency slide, for shame! – Clovenhoof regarded the three stage plan to stop Trump he had jotted on the napkin.

1 – Discredit Trump and his campaign.

2 – Convince him to step down for the sake of the planet (and Topless Darts on Ice).

3 – Terminate with extreme prejudice.

It was a good plan. It was a simple plan. What could go wrong?

Athens, Greece

Michael and Heinz quickly passed through Athens airport as they had only hand luggage. It was warmer than Birmingham by several degrees, and was almost pleasant as they stepped outside, although diesel fumes from an ancient Volvo idling at the kerb filled the air. It was the only vehicle in sight. Michael peered up and down the concourse to see if there might be an obvious place for alternative transport. There was nothing. Michael approached the rusting hulk's driver, who leered through the open window.

"How much to drive us to Avlona?" Michael asked. He spoke impeccable Greek. One of the perks of being a former member of the angelic host was the ability to speak every language of the world impeccably, accentless, and with just a trace of smugness.

"Five hundred euros," answered the driver promptly. "It is a tricky journey. Through the mountains. You must pay in advance."

Michael stepped away and consulted briefly with Heinz, flicking a map up on his phone. "Sounds expensive, but I guess the route isn't as straightforward as it looks on here."

Heinz shrugged.

Michael turned back to the taxi with a sigh, peeled off some notes and climbed into the back. Heinz followed. He had barely closed the door when the taxi screeched away from the kerb. Heinz and Michael tumbled together across the back seat. They struggled upright, Michael scrabbling for his seatbelt. It was trapped, and he was unable to release it.

"Driver! I can't get my seatbelt out. Could you stop please?"

The driver made no indication he had heard. There was a plastic partition separating the front from the back, but surely it wasn't soundproof? Michael tried again.

"Driver! Please stop the car!"

There was no response. The driver tapped the steering wheel rhythmically; Michael realised he was wearing earphones. In horror he watched the driver raise his knees to the steering wheel to free up his hands, pull out his phone and change the music. No! He wasn't just selecting a new tune; he was tapping away like he was engaged in a text conversation. Michael shuffled forward, bracing himself against the constant, violent swerving, and craned his neck . The driver was checking his Facebook feed and playing a video of cats falling off tables. The man's shoulders shook with mirth. Michael banged on the partition, but went unheard. Michael raised his eyes and saw to his horror they were on the wrong side of the carriageway, with a truck bearing down on them. Michael hammered again and shouted as loud as he could. The truck sounded a huge air horn. The driver was oblivious to it all. He pulled a finger across his screen to watch the next video but fumbled his phone, dropping it into the footwell. As he leaned down to retrieve it, he tugged the steering wheel to the side, miraculously avoiding the oncoming truck.

In a frenzy, Michael connected his smartphone to the local phone provider, went onto Facebook, searched for the taxi driver from the name on the printed dashboard plate, sent him a friend request and, when his request was accepted seconds later, wrote on his timeline in big, shouty capitals: *KEEP YOUR EYES ON THE ROAD!* The taxi driver chuckled at that too, although not as much as he did at cat videos.

Michael spent the rest of the journey engaged in frantic prayer to an Almighty he knew on first name terms. Meanwhile Heinz took a nap. They were both slammed back to reality when the taxi slammed into another car, embedding itself firmly in its side. The taxi driver, clearly in the wrong, got out and started to bellow loudly at the driver of the other car. Michael and Heinz took the opportunity to get out of the taxi and stand on trembling legs.

"I wonder how far away we are from Avlona?" said Michael.

Their driver paused in his bellowing and turned to them. "This is Avlona." He gave them a dismissive flick of his hand and went back to shouting and posturing.

"I didn't see any mountains," said Michael, starting to regain his composure. "In fact, would you believe that was only a thirty minute journey? It felt like much, much longer."

Heinz gestured expansively. "Hey, look on the bright side. We're here."

Michael peered at the taxi meter through the passenger window. "We've been well and truly ripped off!"

The taxi driver reached inside his cab and retrieved a wheel brace. He thwacked it against his open palm as he walked towards the other driver.

"Come on!" said Heinz, pulling Michael away. "Let's go and find Aisling."

Michael double checked the address as they approached the building. The sun was setting, and in the low light it resembled many of its neighbours. It was low and white with a flat roof. Close up, he saw that it would be more accurately described as sheets of corrugated iron stacked into a rough cube and whitewashed. A grubby canopy extended perilously onto a pair of spindly props, a scrawny goat glaring at them from its shadow.

There was the sound of someone strumming a guitar and singing. It was a song about figs, apparently.

"Hello Aisling?" called Heinz. "It's Heinz here!"

The guitar stopped. "I don't know anyone called Heinz," called a voice.

"I have pork scratchings and teabags," said Heinz.

There was a clattering sound that could have been a guitar being thrown aside and the creak of corrugated iron.

"Old friend, Jesus, it's grand to see you!" Aisling sprang from a gap and spread her arms wide. She was a wiry woman with an appearance that could be most kindly described as "weathered". She had a rollup clamped between her teeth as she grinned at them.

"This is Michael," said Heinz.

Aisling shook Michael's hand vigorously.

"He's gonna fix Europe, with your help," said Heinz and unpacked the scratchings from his rucksack.

"Don't put them where the goat can get at them," warned Aisling.

"Is he from your goat farm?" asked Michael.

"What?" said Aisling. "This *is* the goat farm."

"I see," said Michael, not really seeing. "Do you have plans to expand at some point? One goat seems very limited for a farm."

"It's the only way to keep within the terms of the subsidy," said Aisling. "The EU gives me money to prove I am limiting the environmental impact of farming. I submit the figures once a year, and they're happy that my goat farm is low impact. If I double my stock they might withdraw funding, and then where would I be?"

"Where indeed?" said Michael, glancing over at the tin shack. "So has Heinz told you about our plan?"

"He has," said Aisling, "and I think it's grand, so. Who's in the band?"

"We need to, er, pick them up," said Michael. He glanced around at the silent street with its weed-strewn verges. "Is there somewhere around here we might get a room for the night? I'll need to sort out some transport for the morning."

Aisling beamed. "I can solve both of those problems for you. With me, lads!"

She led them both to the rear of her shack and Michael saw something whose shape and size was roughly equivalent to a VW camper van. It clearly wasn't an actual vehicle though: there was a wheelbarrow partway up a ramp leading into the back, and the windows were crowded with vegetation.

"You'll need to lend us a hand, boys," said Aisling, as she trotted up the ramp and started loading large potted plants into the barrow. "These'll be safe in the house for a few days, but they're not gonna move themselves, now."

"Is that cannabis?" asked Michael, stepping forward to steady the barrow.

"Sure," said Aisling. "Just a little hobby. You boys can sleep in the back here tonight, and we can set off first thing, yeah?"

"How very rock and roll!" Heinz clapped with delight. "It's a Eurovision tour bus!"

"You settle in," said Aisling. "I'll be taking Jezza to Maria's so she can look after him while we're gone."

"Who's Jezza?" asked Michael. Aisling tied a piece of string around the goat's neck. "You have a goat called Jeremy?"

"And what of it?" said Aisling.

"Nothing," said Michael. "Just I've got a friend called Jeremy. The resemblance is uncanny."

Miami, Florida

A bronze afternoon sun shone into the Miami International airport terminal, even though Clovenhoof's body clock told him it should be dark by now and well past Lambrini o'clock.

"Can you step out of line please, sir," said an immigration official in a smartly pressed, short sleeve shirt.

"I can. I've done it before," said Clovenhoof. He trotted over to the counter to the side of the long queue.

The official clicked his fingers for Clovenhoof to hand his rucksack over. "What is the purpose of your visit to the United States?"

"I've come to see Donald Trump."

The official paused in his ransacking of the rucksack. "See Donald Trump? Are you a Republican, sir?"

"In every sense of the word."

The official took out one of Clovenhoof's bars of Toblerone and sniffed the end. "Are you planning to commit any act of terrorism during your stay in the US?"

If the official had asked if Clovenhoof planned to detonate any explosives or cause widespread alarm, he might have felt honest enough to reply that he was. But bombs and panic did not a terrorist make. Terrorism required beliefs and goals; an agenda. That sounded far too much like hard work to Clovenhoof.

"No."

"Have you ever been to the United States before?"

"No— Oh, yes! Once. Illinois, I think. 1844. To collect one Joseph Smith. I rarely make house calls but he was a special case."

"Joseph Smith?"

"A lying git. Said Eden was in Missouri and that the Almighty lives on a star called Kolob."

The immigration official looked steadily at Clovenhoof. "Are you attempting humour, sir?"

"I've never had to try before."

"Sir, I need to be convinced that you are here for honest and legal reasons."

"You have very beautiful eyes."

"Sir, I have to be satisfied that you do not intend to stay here longer than is allowed and that you do not intend to make the United States your permanent residence."

"Oh, no fear of that. I've a half finished pack of crispy pancakes waiting for me at home. I'm not abandoning them."

"Crispy pancakes?" said the official.

"Don't you have crispy pancakes here?" said Clovenhoof, going ever so slightly weak at his goaty knees. "Thank Findus I brought some with me."

He grabbed his rucksack, rummaged through and produced a smoking jacket, a pair of pants (because one is all you need) and a slightly soggy box of defrosted crispy pancakes. He took one out to show the official. It sagged juicily in Clovenhoof's hands. He was very tempted to scoff it cold.

"Hell is that?" said the man, recoiling, his accent slipping out of a bureaucratic monotone and into something far more regional.

"I think they roam free in the fields of Lincolnshire before they're rounded up and rolled in crumb-crisp coating. Never actually seen one in the wild."

"Please put it away."

Clovenhoof tucked it back in the box and licked his fingers.

"And what is this, sir?" The official held up a miniature bottle of Jim Beam containing a peanut with a horrified face etched on it.

"That is Boris. He's being subjected to extraordinary rendition and will later be put on trial for being a traitor of the highest order and a fatuous cock."

"Sir, this is a peanut," said the official.

"I did say it was extraordinary," argued Clovenhoof.

By the time Clovenhoof had extricated himself from the clutches of US Immigration and Customs and staggered out of to the taxi stand, the sun was setting, the autumn sky was a cloudy grey and it was still hotter than the hottest summer day he'd ever experienced in good old Blighty.

He banged on the roof of the yellow BMW cab at the front of the line. "You free?" he asked.

"No, I charge like everyone else," said the jowly guy in the flat cap behind the wheel.

24

"You'll do," said Clovenhoof and climbed in the front passenger seat.

"Where to, bro?" said the taxi driver.

"I'm here to see Donald Trump."

"Well, he ain't here until tomorrow morning. Where do you want to go meantime, bro? South Beach? The mall? You need somewhere to stay?"

"I do."

"My cousin runs a place off Biscayne Boulevard."

"Will I like it?"

"It has a pool and free Wi-Fi."

"And beds?"

"Sure, bro."

"I'm sold."

"*Bueno*," said the taxi driver and pulled out.

On the elevated expressway into Miami, passing junkyards and shabby bungalows and more palm trees than Clovenhoof had seen since Creation, the driver said, "So, you're a Brit, right?"

"Me? No," said Clovenhoof. "I'm from all over."

"You got the accent, bro."

"All the best villains have a British accent."

"You sound like one of those super-smart guys. Like that Frasier guy."

"I am one of those super-smart guys," Clovenhoof informed him.

The taxi driver gave him a sideways glance. "Bro, you're coming to see Trump. You're not like one of those political commentator guys? Like a professor of elections or something?"

"Indeed I am."

The taxi driver thrust a hand at him, swerving only slightly and drawing angry beeps from other road users. "Mason Miller."

Clovenhoof shook. "Jeremy."

"Bro, my cousin – my other cousin – he's like a producer over at WVLN. It's a two-bit TV station. They've got this evening news spot. I know he'd be super-pleased to get, like, an academic on the show."

"Television?" said Clovenhoof thoughtfully. "I'd need to check my schedule."

He produced his aeroplane napkin and consulted the other side on which he written his Miami plans:

Re-enact series 1 – 3 of Miami vice
Buy a mankini
Strut my funky stuff on the beach
Wrestle an alligator
Trump!

"I could fit it in," he said.

"Super-cool." Mason pulled out a phone and started dialling.

WVLN TV studios occupied a dull, warehouse-like building among many other dull, warehouse-like buildings on an artificial island in the middle of Biscayne Bay. The air-con in reception was cranked up to arctic levels. Clovenhoof shivered while Mason gabbled leisurely with the receptionist before handing Clovenhoof over to a perky young thing with an ID card, a clipboard and a Bluetooth headset.

"How *do* you *do*?" said the perky young thing with such emphasis that it sounded like a genuine question. "I'm Sandee – two *Es* – and I'm so glad you could fit us into your busy schedule. This way please. We're all big fans of you here. Now, it's Dr Jeremy—?"

"Baboon," said Clovenhoof.

Sandee with two *Es* blinked.

"Jeremy Baboon," elaborated Clovenhoof.

"Of course, Dr Baboon."

"Professor."

"Professor Baboon."

"Sir."

"Sir?"

Clovenhoof whipped on a pair of intelligent-looking spectacles he had brought along. "Sir Professor Jeremy Baboon of the London College of Arms," he said, popping a large briar pipe he had also brought along between his lips. Clovenhoof always carried a pipe with him: in case he found something interesting to smoke, or needed it to gesticulate in an authoritative and intellectual manner. It was surprising how effective it was.

"Your ... your majesty?" said Sandee, bewildered. She managed a little curtsey, despite the confines of the elevator they were in.

"No need for that," he said. "On meeting a knight of the realm, one only needs to bow one's head. *Facilius fellatio*, my dear." He smiled magnanimously.

Sandee bowed.

Clovenhoof was rushed through to make-up where an unfortunate fellow tried to match Clovenhoof's red skin tones to his palette of foundations and blushers. The fellow gave up and just gave Clovenhoof's hair a touch of gel. He stabbed himself on one of Clovenhoof's horns and couldn't figure for the life of him why his hand was bleeding.

In the studio (which Clovenhoof decided was not half as big as a TV studio ought to be even though he'd never been in one before), he was miked up and left to sit quietly while the anchorwoman, Summer Hanrahan, did a piece to camera.

"...and asked if he regretted the tattoo, the Boward resident said 'Ted Cruz is a personal and national hero and seeing his face every day gives me the will and strength to go on with life.'" Summer Hanrahan turned to another camera for no discernible reason. "Republican presidential candidate, Donald Trump, is in Miami tomorrow to meet supporters at Bayfront Park. With exactly a week to go before the nation decides, the latest ABC polls show Trump one point ahead of Hillary Clinton. To discuss the impact of this poll, and how the two presidential hopefuls are perceived on the international stage, we are joined by Sir Professor Jeremy Baboon of the London College of Arms." She turned to Clovenhoof with a little bow of her head. "Sir Jeremy."

"Summer," he grinned.

"First, I have to say the people of the United States are full of admiration for the British people and your recent Brexit: freeing yourself from European control. The future's looking bright, would you say?"

"Well, Summer, the fight for Brexit was a long and arduous one. As you know, Nigel Farage, personal friend of Mr Trump and official leader of Her Majesty's opposition, had an uphill battle. Like the Spartan heroes of old, he and his small, plucky band stood at the gates of Dover; the liberal élite cowering behind him, the amassed foreign hordes in front of him. There they stood, bare-chested, nipples proud, and with a yell of 'This! Is! Sparta!' took back control of the country from the sausage and garlic munching eurocrats of Brussels. It truly was a blow to the establishment."

"And do you think that Donald Trump – a man who has never held public office – can deliver a similar knockout blow to the political establishment in Washington?"

Clovenhoof gesticulated with his pipe in an authoritative and intellectual manner. "Donald Trump has, like Nigel Farage, set himself up as an outsider and champion of the underdog. The people need a champion: one who thinks how they think, feels what they feel; one who knows the hardships of small town, Middle America and knows what it is like to be downtrodden by Big Government."

"That they do," nodded Summer.

"And who could be a better champion than New York billionaire, Democrat donor and TV host, Donald Trump: a man who built a financial empire with nothing but his two hands and the hundreds of millions of dollars he inherited from his father."

"Do you think we can trust the polls?" asked Summer.

"Oh, you hear some horror stories but most of them are lovely people," said Clovenhoof. "I had one come do my bathroom this year. Piotr worked all hours of the day, never took a break and made a superb job of the grouting, including that tricky bit behind the power shower."

"I'm not sure I understand..."

"And I think Donald Trump's decision to focus on immigration in his campaign is a brave decision."

"Do you feel that he is simply voicing what many Americans feel?"

"I do. And it's very brave. Here is a man willing to say exactly what people want to hear. The American people want to find an external cause for all their problems. They want someone to say: it's not your fault, none of it's your fault. It's the fault of the Mexicans and the Muslims and the blacks."

"African-Americans, professor."

"Of course. I was just quoting the great man himself. The Americans want a Führer who will tell them none of it is their fault, that all their problems are caused by others and who will lull the electorate to sleep with his hollow promises. And Donald Trump is absolutely that man, and he's willing to say those things even though he is a Muslim woman from Mexico."

Summer Hanrahan froze for a split second. She looked at camera one, camera two, her notes and then back to Clovenhoof. "He is a what, professor?"

"A Muslim woman from Mexico."

"Donald Trump...?"

Clovenhoof gave an extra-special authoritative and intellectual wave of his pipe. "As part of our work at the London College of Arms, we've researched the family trees of every US president and, presumptuous perhaps—" he chuckled, "—we took a cursory peek at that of Donald Trump. Or, I should say, Dina al Trompeta."

"Dina..."

"... al Trompeta," nodded Clovenhoof. "Lovely name. Literally translates as 'Love the trumpet' which is beautiful in and of itself. I think it's a shame that a young Mexican woman of the Islamic faith, knowing she will face prejudice and suspicion all her life, has to make the hardest of decisions to transform herself into a privileged white man in order to make any headway in life. It's a shame, Summer."

Summer laughed. She laughed to give herself a moment to think. She laughed because Clovenhoof's assertion was patently ridiculous. She laughed because the alternative was to cry.

"Forgive me, professor, but I find it hard to believe that Donald J Trump is actually – was ever – a Mexican. Or a Muslim. Or a woman?"

"You think such a thing is beyond the abilities of Trump – I mean Trompeta?" said Clovenhoof. "You think that it is impossible for a woman to become whatever she wants to be? Do you think

Rosa Park sat on that bus all those years ago just so you could tell another woman what she can or cannot do?"

"I don't think..." said Summer faltering.

"Clearly," said Clovenhoof. "We should celebrate, not decry our Republican candidate for being a proud Muslim Mexican woman. Proud? Yes. We know how much he loves tacos on Cinco de Mayo. And he's told us so many times that he has many Muslim friends. Of course he does. He is one. So we can't call him a racist because now we know that when we hear talk of a great wall along our southern borders, or a blanket ban on Muslims entering the country, Trompeta is talking about his own people."

Summer had a finger to her ear, apparently listening to a voice from the production box. "Professor, what proof do you have of this?" she asked.

"Proof?" said Clovenhoof.

"You discovered that Trump is a ... is something other than he appears to be."

"I don't know, but a lot of people are saying it."

"A lot of people are saying it?"

Clovenhoof nodded enthusiastically. "A lot of people are saying that Trump is nothing more than a Latino Muslim honey in disguise. A lot of people."

"But you said you had found out that Trump was a Mexican."

"That's what I'm hearing, Summer. And I think it's up to Trump to prove to us that he's not. Have you seen his birth certificate?"

"Er, no."

Clovenhoof threw his arms wide in surprise. "Why is that? I've not seen it; you've not seen it. What's he got to hide? It's very suspicious. And we're hearing that he founded ISIS, which is starting to make sense now, isn't it?"

"Is it?" said Summer. "I thought we were talking about his birth certificate?"

A frantic looking man behind the camera was making equally frantic 'wind it up' gestures to Summer.

"It's all a web of lies," said Clovenhoof. "The lack of a birth certificate. His lesbian marriage. His involvement with 7-Eleven."

"You mean 9/11?"

"He was involved in 9/11? I'm glad you can confirm that because I've been hearing a lot about that. True fact: on 9/11, Trump called up a television station to tell them that when the twin towers fell, his own building was now the tallest in Manhattan! What more proof do you need?"

"Proof of what?"

"Summer!" he screamed. "Wake up and smell the jihad! We don't even have proof he was ever born!"

And then the red lights went out on the cameras and a door was flung open from the production box and all manner of shouting and swearing broke loose. As Clovenhoof was hurried out of the WVLN studio, there was more swearing; even an inexpertly thrown milkshake from a band of irate and fleet-footed members of the public. Clovenhoof was bundled into the back of Mason Miller's yellow cab.

Mason whooped as his tyres spun and he accelerated out of the studio parking lot. "That was amazing! I watched it all in reception."

"Everyone seemed surprisingly angry," Clovenhoof observed, licking strawberry milkshake off his professorial glasses.

"I don't know why, bro," said Mason. "That station's audience amounts to two seniors and their pet Chihuahua, but you roused up a lynch mob. They might be pissed today, but they'll be smiling at their ratings tomorrow. And that look on Summer's face, bro. Super-cool."

"Thanks," said Clovenhoof.

"So, is it true?" asked Mason.

"What?"

"What you said in there? About Trump?"

Clovenhoof shrugged. "What is truth, Mason? Hmmm? What is truth?"

"That's deep, bro," said Mason and drove on into the evening.

2nd November 2016

Tuna Apartments, Mason's other cousin's place off Biscayne Boulevard, was a faded and peeling hotel with, as promised, a pool, free Wi-Fi and beds. Clovenhoof had paid for the room, tipped Mason heavily, and told him to come back at eight sharp the following morning.

Clovenhoof woke in the night. At least it was night in Miami but Clovenhoof's infernal internal clock insisted it was daytime and he should be about his wicked work. He lay on top of his sheets, trying to will himself back to sleep. He tried counting damned souls in his head. He tried to remember the names of all the angels who had stood with him against the Almighty. He tried whacking himself on the head with the bedside lamp and, when that failed, holding his breath until he passed out. However, jetlag, the southern heat and the broiling contents of his stomach (four crispy pancakes and two leaden pounds of Halloween candy) kept him awake.

Defeated, he got up, wandered to the window and by chance happened to see, by the pink neon light of the hotel sign, the long-haired man in flip-flops and a bathrobe down by the pool, poking the water. Intrigued and bored in equal measure, Clovenhoof stepped out onto his balcony. He could hear the engines of passing traffic, mingled with the sounds of a city with a million air-conditioners. He descended the metal steps to the poolside.

The long-haired man, a roll-up clenched between his lips, was sprinkling various gobbets and drops from a squeezy pipette into the pool, stirring them with his fingers.

"What are you doing?" said Clovenhoof.

The man stumbled, spat out his roll-up in surprise, almost falling into the pool after it. "Damn it, dude!" he snapped. "Where'd you spring from?"

"Spring? Nowhere. I merely am."

The long-haired man ignored him while he fished in the pool for his roll-up. With an "Ah-hah!" he caught it and, rather optimistically, was about to put the damp slug of a thing back in his mouth when he gave Clovenhoof a suspicious glance. "You a cop, dude?"

"Nope," said Clovenhoof.

"Fed? CIA? NSA? You have to tell me if you are."

"I'm none of those things," said Clovenhoof. "I'm more of a bad guy."

"You swear?"

"I solemnly swear I am up to no good," said Clovenhoof, fingers raised in the Boy Scout salute.

The man had to hold the spliff up with three supporting fingers just to get it straight. He knew he was onto a loser before he even attempted to relight it. He laid it aside on the concrete to dry and, with another suspicious glance at Clovenhoof, went into the little pouch strapped to his waist and pulled out the weed, tobacco and papers to roll a new one.

"In Britain, they call those bum bags," said Clovenhoof, conversationally.

"Do they?"

"Amazingly, fanny pack sounds even more stupid than bum bag. First time I heard someone talking about their fanny pack I thought they had a deck of porno playing cards."

"I don't get it."

"See? That's what cannabis does to your mind. What you doing anyway?" Clovenhoof pointed at the smears of liquid and powder the man had dropped in the pool.

"Can you keep a secret?"

"I'm sure it's entirely possible."

"This—" he gestured to the pool and the plastic tubs and chemical bottles in front of him "—is 'Francis Jackson's plan to save life on Planet Earth', cos let me tell you, this planet is fucked with a capital..." He stopped, licked his fresh spliff and inserted it between his lips. "Did I say 'fucked' or 'screwed'?"

"Fucked."

"Capital *F*," said Francis. He lit his spliff and took a deep drag before offering it to Clovenhoof.

Clovenhoof obliged. It was a sweet and calming head-rush but it wasn't a patch on a half-bottle of Lambrini.

"You know what life is?" said Francis.

"God's greatest mistake?"

"Ha! True dat. Life is just chemicals. Proteins and molecules and shit floating in the primordial sea."

"Ah. And this is you creating life?"

"Still tweaking the formula, dude. But once I've got it, I'm bottling it up and then, when all the nuclear winter shit has blown over, we can start afresh. Birds, insects, fish, elephants. Hey, you wanna know a fact about elephants?"

"Do I ever!"

"This is a fact. A true fact. The CIA and Secret Service can't detect elephants."

Clovenhoof considered this. Francis dropped a lump of something spongey into the pool. Neon ripples spread out from the point of impact.

"You don't believe me," said Francis. "Dude, it's true."

"The Secret Service can't detect elephants?"

"Trust me. I work with them."

"The Secret Service or elephants?"

"Elephants, dude," he said, slapping Clovenhoof's shoulder. "I work over at Florida Safari Gardens in Sarasota. I'm just over here visiting my girl for a couple of days. I'm doing my doctoral thesis while I'm there. You want hooking up with a midnight elephant ride or a gnu – we got the best gnus – then I'm your man."

"And the Secret Service can't detect them? I only ask because elephants are, you know, kind of big."

"Right. Right," said Francis. "They're tall but the spooks are trained to spot threats at head height. Elephants are above all that. And their body density. The thermal imagers and the body scanners can't read them. The elephant's body fucks with 'em. They think the elephant's a tree or some shit."

"A big grey walking tree."

"Right."

"With tusks."

"You got it, dude." Francis regarded his spent spliff, took a last drag on it and looked at his pool polluting experiments. "This planet's fucked," he said softly. "The country's going to hell."

"You never know. Clinton might win."

Francis snorted and tossed the dog-end into the pool. "I'm voting for Trump, dude."

Clovenhoof was genuinely surprised. "Really? You sound like a smart guy. You look kind of ... liberal."

"You could paint me commie red if you liked, dude. I would have voted for Bernie Sanders if he was on the Democrat ticket but, in a choice between Clinton and Trump, I'm gonna have to vote for Trump."

"Okay. You've definitely been smoking too much pot."

"No way, dude. That's a physical impossibility." Francis switched out from his crouch and dangled his feet in the pool. After a moment, Clovenhoof did the same and dipped his hoofs in the water. "This country needs a big shake up," said Francis. "Clinton. She's just gonna be four more years of the same old shit."

"Cheap healthcare and gay rights," said Clovenhoof.

"And special interest groups. Trade agreements that cost jobs. Drone strikes on civilian populations. Democracy is a joke but, you know what: Trump's in on the joke. American politics – all of America, period – is a 24/7 rolling reality TV show, except recently it's turning into *This Is Spinal* fucking *Tap* and Donald Trump is the star."

"So, you're going to vote for him because he's entertaining?"

"Kill or cure, dude. If we need to have a revolution to get our country back to what it once was, maybe what it never was but we always wanted it to be, then President Trump is the man to get the ball rolling. He's like—" Francis hesitated and grabbed at the air as if he could pull his lost thoughts back down. "Like – fuck! Who's that dude? A voice crying in the wilderness dude."

"Bear Grylls?"

"Dude from the Bible. Ate locusts and honey."

"John the Baptist."

"Right!"

"The man was a nutter," said Clovenhoof. "Trust me. Spent his days dunking people in the river and telling them that God forgave them. Who knew you could get into the Almighty's good books with a quick wash? So Trump's John the Baptist, is he? You know things didn't end well for old John?"

"You think I care? Trump is a vile racist thug who thinks sexually assaulting chicks is just swell and groovy. He's just the catalyst. At least with him, what you see is what you get. He wears his stupids on his sleeve."

Francis raised his gaze to the road beyond the hotel grounds. There was a breeze in the air – not cool, just the same static warm as the pool water and the concrete. Off in the distance, there was the vaguest suggestion of a coming dawn.

"I've got to muck out the tiger in a couple of hours," he said. "Might need to get my head straight before I do that."

He opened his fanny pack drugs kits, considered it for a goodly long while (during which Clovenhoof suspected he actually dozed off for half a second) and then decided that, tempting though it was, going into a tiger cage while high was not the smart choice.

"Yep," he said, closed the bag and looked at Clovenhoof. "Well, it was nice to meet you, Professor Baboon."

"Saw that, did you?" said Clovenhoof, smiling.

"I reckon Trump's not the only one who's in on the joke, huh? You know what I think a man like you could use?" He waved a sealed plastic bag that looked like it was full of brown turds.

"Shit biscuits?" said Clovenhoof.

"Snacks for the ultimate road trip, dude. My own blend of mom's chocolate brownie recipe and thirty mils of top grade acid."

"For when life just ain't trippy enough?"

"Right on, dude," said Francis.

Clovenhoof gave it some serious thought. "Do you take credit cards?" he asked.

Avlona, Greece

Michael's initial assessment of the van's roadworthiness didn't change much once it was moving. They careered precariously along the northbound motorway, through rolling countryside with a surface layer of green and an underlying terrain resembling something left in the oven too long. Michael was determined to check the tyres when he got a chance, because it felt as if they were all flat. According to Aisling some of the gears could only be engaged when the van was going downhill, which meant they spent much of the travelling time subjected to a migraine-inducing whine from an over-revving engine. Or a bone-shuddering vibration, permanently on the verge of bringing them to a stop but never quite making it. At least, reflected Michael, they were in Aisling's hands rather than the psychotic taxi driver's. Aisling seemed to understand something about keeping on the correct side of the carriageway, even if her attention was prone to wandering as she contemplated the song that she needed to write.

"So guys, we need an amazing song. I've been working on a little thing about figs."

"Figs," said Michael.

"They are amazing, don't you think? They grow on trees and you can just pick them, yet they're *so sweet*."

"That's perhaps a little specific to your own experience," said Michael carefully. "I'd imagined to bring Europe together we'd want something a bit more universal."

"Who doesn't love a fig?" said Aisling. "Anyway, it's a song with a message. Get a load of this." She sang, in a high and melodious voice:

"Fig tree, my lovely fig tree.
"Nobody could ever accuse you of bigotry."

Michael was briefly dumbstruck. Aisling's Celtic brogue and the delicate tune she'd applied made it sound beautiful, and it did carry a hint of the sentiment that he was after, but...

"No," said Michael. "Figs are just not right."

Perhaps he was being old fashioned, perhaps he remembered that the Son of God had not been a fan of figs, cursing them left right and centre, but even in this day and age figs would not do. He cleared his throat and switched on his tablet.

"As it happens, I have done some research on this. I'm sure someone of your song-writing calibre can take this on board and use it." He tapped the screen. "I have analysed past winners and you will not be surprised that the majority of them are in English."

"Yep, English would have been my—"

"However, there are other languages that have won, so it might be prudent to include some of those as well."

"A multi-lingual song?" said Aisling stiffly.

"Absolutely. You will want to include snippets of French, Dutch, Hebrew, German, Norwegian, Swedish, Italian, Spanish, Danish, Ukrainian, Croatian, Serbian and Crimean Tatar."

"All of them?" said Aisling through gritted teeth.

"Now, it stands to reason that each language should be represented in proportion to the amount of times it has provided a winner. So, while one minute and twenty-three seconds of the song will be in English, for example, you will only need two point seven seconds of Crimean Tatar based on—"

"*I'm not so sure,*" Heinz interrupted loudly from the back, "that Aisling's on board with the multi-language approach."

"But it's integral to my entire plan," said Michael.

"*I remember* Liam mentioning a little twitch she gets at the corner of her eye, just before Aisling has one of her episodes."

Michael gave the Irishwoman a fearful look. Her hands were gripping the steering wheel with white-knuckle intensity. "Episodes?" he said, voice hoarse.

"Post-traumatic stress," said Aisling. "I once had a boyfriend who, as they used to say, 'done me wrong'. He was trilingual, Swiss. Now I can't hear two languages squashed up close together without the red mist descending."

"I will make a note of that," said Michael and shuffled a few inches further away from her.

"So, what else you got, Michael? Any other songwriting tips for the girl who wrote more Eurovision winners than anyone in history?"

Michael eyed her. "It will keep until later, I'm sure."

They travelled for an hour or two without further comment, through terrain that was increasingly green and less over-cooked. Michael became aware that Heinz was exploring the back of the van. At some point in the past it had been fitted with cupboards.

"Hey, this is pretty cool: there's a tiny stove, and a thing which looks like a heater."

"That would have been worth knowing last night," said Michael, remembering how chilly he'd been, stretched out listening to Heinz snoring.

"The heater runs on diesel directly from the fuel tank," said Aisling. "Can't have you wasting it keeping warm, so. We want to get to Sofia today, don't we lads?"

"Maybe we should get some sleeping bags then," sulked Michael. "We can't make great art if we're all sleep deprived."

Miami, Florida

Wednesday. Presidential hopeful Donald J Trump made his first public appearance of the day at a warm but windy Bayfront Park in Miami. Standing at a podium with a massive star spangled banner behind him, Trump told his supporters not to get complacent because the polls showed he was ahead.

"The polls are all saying we're gonna win Florida," he said. "Don't believe it. Don't believe it. Get out there and vote. Pretend we're slightly behind."

"What the buggering blue blazes is wrong with his hair?" said Clovenhoof, watching him speak from the back rows of the amphitheatre.

"How can you say that?" said Mason the cabbie.

"I mean, it looks like a thousand ginger toms all just moulted on top of his head and he thought, 'Mmmm, this looks good. I'll keep it.' It literally looks like it's trying to escape or evolve or something."

"I mean, how can you say that considering what you got on your head?"

"Surely, Ah don't know what you mean, suh," said Clovenhoof in his best southern belle falsetto, and adjusted his blonde wig. In addition to the wig, Clovenhoof was wearing a large floral maternity dress, covering the plump breasts and pregnancy bump he had artfully constructed out of hotel pillows and towels. "And Ah'll thank you to kindly keep your eyes up here," he told Mason. "A true gentleman should never ogle a lady's bazongas."

"Your bazongas came from the hotel bathroom, bro," said Mason. "And you'd better return them when you're done. What you doing anyhow?"

"This," said Clovenhoof, waving his arms. "Donald! Donald!" he called out. "Why don't you return my calls no more? Donald!"

Clovenhoof strode out towards the distant podium, waving and hollering. He was too far away for the septuagenarian Trump to hear, but members of the crowd looked at him and some of the TV news crews who hadn't secured decent spots near the front started turning their cameras.

Clovenhoof held his weighty eight-months-gone bump and waddled with affected difficulty towards the stage. "It's your baby, Donald! It's yours! Why won't you acknowledge it? Do you want me to have one of them ungodly abortions?"

There were some nearby boos; an elderly man made a disgusted shooing gesture at him. Two earpiece-wearing men emerged seamlessly from the crowd to block Clovenhoof's path. One moment they weren't there, the next they were; impressive since both were about seven feet tall and build like rugby forwards.

"You can't come through here, ma'am," said one.

"But Ah need to speak to my Donald! He needs to face up to his responsibilities."

"You need to vacate this area, ma'am," said the other.

"Won't y'all allow a fine southern gal speak to the man who made her with child?" said Clovenhoof, half-appealing to the crowd.

"Ma'am, you need to go back the way you came."

Seeing that his obvious charms were having no effect on the secret service guys, Clovenhoof decided on another tactic. With a cry of "Oh, lordy," he threw up his hands and fell into a faint into one of the men's arms.

They lowered Clovenhoof to the ground. One secret service agent put a finger to his ear and hissed, "Control. This is Eyeline Two. We have a pregnant woman collapsed in the north section. Repeat: pregnant woman is down."

The secret service agent listened for a moment. Clovenhoof lay limp.

"No, Pregnant Woman is not code for Mike Pence. Mike Pence is codename Hoosier. We have a pregnant woman." He listened. "No. No. Not Hooters. No one is codename Hooters."

"JFK," said the other agent.

"What?"

"JFK. 1960 election. Codename Hooters, I swear."

"That is not helpful." Finger to the earpiece again. "Control we have an actual pregnant woman collapsed in the north section. A pregnant woman. Code? Dammit, Kyle. We don't have a code for a fainted pregnant woman."

Through half-open eyes, Clovenhoof could see a crowd was gathering around him. It was odd but true that a person lying perfectly still on the floor drew more attention that a disturbingly masculine pregnant woman waving and shouting hysterically.

Clovenhoof's eyes fluttered open. "Oh, my," he sighed. "Did Ah faint?"

"Let me help you up, ma'am," said a secret service agent.

"Well, bless your heart, young man." Clovenhoof came to his feet unsteadily, making sure his wig was still in place.

"Debbie Li, Channel Twelve News." A woman thrust a microphone in Clovenhoof's face. "Can you tell me what happened?"

"Oh, Ah am so embarrassed," said Clovenhoof demurely. "This little one is so heavy. Ah shouldn't be out in my condition. Ah would not be surprised if he shot out right now with all the excitement."

"Let's hope that doesn't happen," said the other secret service guy with a note of genuine fear in his voice.

"Ah'm going to call him Donald John, after his daddy. DJ for short."

"Are you saying you are pregnant with Trump's child?" said Debbie Li from Channel Twelve News.

"That Ah am, honey-pie."

"We can't do this interview here," said the agent.

"First amendment rights," said Debbie Li with hardnosed ferocity. "Ted, get a tight shot on her," she told her cameraman.

"Ah don't want to cause no fuss now," said Clovenhoof.

"You're not causing no fuss," said Debbie Li. "You tell us your story in your own words."

"Well, it was—" Clovenhoof quickly counted on his fingers "—It was February and Donnie – Ah call him Donnie – came by my daddy's place. He was canvassing. We're grand ol' party people, real

Republican supporters. And Donnie came calling and we asked him to sit a spell on the veranda."

The secret service guy was talking in his earpiece again. "Control, Eyeline Two. We have a Magpie in the north section. Magpie in the north section."

"Ah, could see that Donnie had taken a fancy to me," said Clovenhoof. "When we were introduced, he couldn't keep his tiny little hands off of me."

"No," hissed the agent. "Not an actual magpie. Press intrusion! It's code for press intrusion, Kyle! Godammit man!"

"And what happened then?" asked the Channel Twelve reporter.

"Well, daddy and Donnie had some business to discuss but Donnie came looking for me." Clovenhoof dabbed at the non-existent tears on his cheeks. "And then he grabbed me by my ... by my special place."

"Your special place?" said Debbie Li, horrified.

"Uh-huh. The old cypress tree down by the bayou where we have the swing. He grabbed me by the cypress tree and held me close and he said, 'Mary-Pam—' Mary-Pam he called me because that's my name '—Mary-Pam, Ah ain't nothing but a low down dog but Ah want you and, even though Ah am married and it is a sin against God in Heaven, Ah will have my wicked way with you.' And he did."

The crowd gasped.

"He had sexual relations with you?" said Debbie Li.

"Oh, Ah am so ashamed, Debbie. Ah knew it was wrong. But Ah let him do it, even though he had done it to my two sisters, Mary-Sue and Mary-Lou before me."

"Your two sisters?"

"Three of us in a row in one afternoon. Wham, bam, thank you Pam. But he promised he'd do right by all of us. We were going to go to Utah and get one of them polygamous weddings even though we ain't Mormons nor nothing. But he abandoned us and Ah am here today to make sure he supports us. Ah am sure there'd be room for all of us in the White House."

"You think Trump is going to win the presidency? After what he did."

"Sure, honey-pie, even though he's been grabbing woman after woman in their special places and spreading his adulterous seed all over the Deep South, Trump is the only one who will see a return to those traditions and moral values that everyone associates with good ol' Dixie. The South will rise again!"

The members of the public around Clovenhoof were variously appalled, angry, confused and fascinated. A couple cheered. Barely anyone within sight was paying any attention to the presidential candidate on the podium. There were now at least three news teams gathered round Clovenhoof, and he was thinking it couldn't be going any better, when a loud voice from the nearby seats said, "Hey! Aren't you that Professor Baboon ass off the TV?"

Clovenhoof looked at a fat round face attached to fat round body which was attached to a gallon-sized cup of soda. Clovenhoof recalled the fat face and fat body hurling a cup of strawberry milkshake at him the previous night.

"He's a man in a dress!" yelled fat face.

Clovenhoof quickly grabbed the man's soda and emptied it over his own crotch. "Oh, my! My waters have broken!"

"Ted, can you get a close-up on that?"

"Control, we're gonna need an ambulance down here. Lady's about to give birth."

"Ah am about to produce a little Trump."

"Give her some air! And an exclusive interview contract!"

"No, Kyle! It is not code!"

"Ah can feel it coming! Where's Donnie? Donnie! Your baby's coming!"

"Don't push! Don't push!"

The crowd rippled as a pair of very prompt paramedics pushed through. People stood. The crowd swelled. And by the time the paramedics reached the spot there was nothing there but a gaggle of camera crews, an apoplectic secret service guy and a discarded blonde wig.

"You look pleased with yourself, bro," said Mason as he drove the getaway cab from Bayfront Park.

"Indeed I am," said Clovenhoof from the back seat. He shuffled out of his dress and delivering himself of a bouncy baby pillow. "I've labelled the champion of the ultra-conservative right as a love-cheat and ravisher of virginal Christian ladies."

"And where was that virginal Christian lady meant to be from? Your accent was..."

"A bit all over?"

"From another century, bro."

"Doesn't matter. I've sullied the man's character. Just watch his popularity tumble."

"If you say so. You fancy some breakfast, bro? You like Dunkin' Donuts?"

"I don't know. I've never dunked one before."

"Then it's settled," said Mason and turned west towards the golden autumn sun and the sea. "Donuts are the best. I tell you, bro. Every day I get down on my knees and thank God for the gift of donuts."

Sofia, Bulgaria

Michael jolted awake from a dream where souls in torment howled for mercy. Heinz had picked up Aisling's guitar and was strumming chords and more words to the fig song.

"When I think back on all the fig trees I've known

"I know in my heart I'll never be alone"

Michael winced at Heinz's coarse voice. "I thought we were dropping the figs? Anyway, it's essential we don't mention hearts in the song. Nine of the lowest placed acts since the turn of the century have performed songs about hearts. It's the strongest characteristic shared by losing songs."

"And how many of those losers sang songs about figs, Michael?" asked Aisling with a steely glare. "It's none, isn't it? You have no evidence that a fig song couldn't be a winner."

Michael closed his eyes and went back to sleep.

He woke for a second time as the van rattled over cobblestones. "Is this Sofia?" he asked, peering out at a street market piled with fresh vegetables, nuts and honey.

"It is indeed," said Aisling. "And where now are we going to find our man? This address seems to be something like a plaza. It's just up here."

"I think we'll know him when we see him," said Michael.

Aisling parked the van near a café. They all climbed out, grateful for the chance to stretch their legs.

"Let's get a drink and something to eat while we work out how to find Todor," said Michael, heading for a café table. He sat and looked around. The café filled a corner of the plaza, commanding a view of a square crowded by the market. Stallholders vied for the attention of a dwindling afternoon crowd.

"*Tri kafeta, molya*," Michael said to the waiter before casting about the square. "Right, let's see who can be first to spot our future Eurovision champion. Who wants to go first?"

Heinz leaned forward, gave an exaggerated wink and whispered conspiratorially. "I like the kids with the skateboard. They've got some amazing moves. We use them for the video, yes?"

They all watched a pair of youths, skating across the top of the steps of a stern Soviet-era building. One jumped, flicking the skateboard up with him and rode down the metal handrail onto the cobbles.

"Gnarly nosegrind," said Aisling as the lads disappeared behind some of the market stalls, all the while maintaining a look of studied insouciance.

"They've got talent," said Heinz. "But they need a haircut, yes?"

"Video. I hadn't thought about a video," mused Michael.

Heinz choked briefly on his coffee. "Seriously? You want to win over the hearts and minds of Europe and you hadn't thought about a video? I have ideas. Many ideas, but they could be expensive."

Aisling looked intently around the square, sucking her teeth. "There is very little poetry in this place. I can't begin to imagine the visuals for our fig song."

"It's not a fig song," said Michael.

"Our ... song then," said Aisling. "If your man over there would pack in those godawful Disney tunes, I might be able to think for a moment."

Michael and Heinz looked at the stallholder who was upsetting Aisling. He was a barrel-chested young man in a bow tie, a grocer's apron and a fat moustache. His stall seemed to sell nothing but tomatoes: ranging from tiny cherry ones still on the vine to enormous beef tomatoes the size of a baby's head. All the while he beamed at passers-by and sang in a high-pitched disco diva voice.

"What *is* that song that he's singing, though?" said Michael. He struggled to place it before realising Aisling was right. "It is a Disney song."

"*Beauty and the Beast* or *Tale as Old as Time*. Ashman and Menken. 1991," said Aisling.

Michael listened closer. "Does he have a drum machine under that stall?"

Heinz leap to his feet and started to dance. "It's kind of cool," he said, strutting between the tables like a pale, pot-bellied John Travolta.

Michael couldn't keep the smug grin from his face. Aisling looked at him and groaned. "You're feckin' kidding me!"

"No," said Michael.

"The falsetto with a Bontempi organ?"

"Trust the algorithms."

Miami, Florida

Knowing his Stateside mission was done, Clovenhoof spent the rest of the day ticking off items on his Miami To Do list. He bought a white suit, pushed his sleeves up Eighties style, rented a speedboat and cruised up and down the bay, singing the Miami Vice theme song and trying to arrest tourists for being "drug-dealing scum". Then he switched the suit for a leopard print mankini and walked the length of Miami Beach, making sure all the women (short, tall, young and old, because Clovenhoof was an equal opportunities arsehole) got a salacious wink, a good look at his package and a double entendre.

Pleased with his accomplishments, Clovenhoof returned to the Tuna Apartments and turned on the television to see how the mighty Trump had been brought down by an evening and a morning of Satanic mischief making.

As night fell, Francis, the friendly neighbourhood zookeeper, drug-dealer and recreational life creator, knocked at Clovenhoof's door and entered to find the devil sat on his bed, surrounded by several dozen Halloween candy wrappers, forlornly scrolling through news channel after news channel.

"Brought your order, dude." Francis placed a baggie of acid brownies on the nightstand. "Put my business card in there in case you need a re-order." He looked at all the wrappers. "Got the munchies?"

"I've been eating nothing but sweets and cold pancakes for two days," said Clovenhoof. "My colon is more bunged up than the M6 at rush hour. Thought shoving more in might encourage things to move along." He sighed very heavily. "I'm also eating because I'm depressed."

"Dude," said Francis sympathetically.

"You saw me on TV last night. I was scintillating. And this morning, I pulled a full blown one woman protest at Trump's rally. I've accused him live on air of being a woman, a 9/11 conspirator, an illegal immigrant and impregnating three sisters in one afternoon. I tore the man to pieces. And is it on the news? Is it? Is it?" Clovenhoof continued to flick through TV channels. "It's just soundbites from Trump about Clinton and this e-mail server. I don't even understand what that's got to do with anything."

"You were on WVLN last night," said Francis, as though that explained everything.

"Yes. And?"

"Well, maybe you didn't know WVLN is affiliated to a certain global news corporation whose bosses are buddies with Trump."

"What?" Clovenhoof was confused. "You mean they played it down because they didn't agree with it?"

"They'll have buried any anti-Trump story you might have been part of, dude. And your protest today, unless you were being filmed by Channel Nuebe, will be buried too."

"Well that's a floating turd in the swimming lane of my life," said Clovenhoof, disgusted. "And I put on my best dress and everything!"

"You can't directly attack Trump through the broadcast media. The right wing has that sewn up every place west of New England and east of California. You could prove Trump injects heroin into puppies' eyeballs and you wouldn't dissuade the voters. He's beyond that. Dude, folks are gonna vote for him because of what they expect him to *do*. Everything he's done, nobody cares."

"Then how do I stop him?" demanded Clovenhoof sulkily, punching the bed and sending candy wrappers everywhere.

"Stop him?" Francis scratched the stubble on his chin. "The man's a force of nature. I think he's untouchable." Something in Clovenhoof's pathetically pouty face made Francis sit down and pat the downcast devil on the back. "Don't worry, dude. Speaking as someone who's voting for the man, he's not going to win. Not really."

"But you said..."

"Mine's a protest vote, dude. Ninety percent of Trump's supporters are racist rednecks who can take their mom, aunt and sister out for dinner at the same time and only need a table for two. The other ten percent are the jokers, the assholes and the counter-culture terrorists like myself. And even if we all voted for Trump, he'd have no chance against Hillary unless *millions* of perfectly ordinary rational Americans – Hispanics, African-Americans, women for God's sake – switched to his side."

"Oh," said Clovenhoof, slightly mollified.

"Soo, dude, if you really want to nix Trump's chances, you know, just to be sure, then you just need to remind those wavering voter what kind of swivel-eyed inbreds their fellow Trump supporters are."

"Make members of the public look stupid?" said Clovenhoof. "I can do that. Where's the next Trump rally?"

"He's here, there and everywhere, dude," said Francis.

Clovenhoof searched the internet on his phone and then called Mason.

"I'm going to need your services tomorrow. We're driving to Charlotte. North Carolina." Clovenhoof looked round for an uneaten candy bar as Mason's voice went up an octave. "Okay," said Clovenhoof. "So it's a ten hour drive. Better be here nice and early." He hung up.

"So, dude," said Francis, "I was gonna go get some chicken wings. Maybe Hooters down in Bayside Marketplace. You coming?"

"Sure," said Clovenhoof, rolling off the bed and onto his hoofs. "Did you know, Hooters was JFK's secret service codename?"

"Kennedy's codename was Hooters?"

"Secret service guy told me," said Clovenhoof, grabbing his door key.

"Figures."

Carpathian Mountains, Romania

Todor, the young Bulgarian tomato seller turned Eurovision hopeful, visibly sagged with relief when they crossed the unmanned border into Romania.

"Happy to give up the tomato selling life?" Michael asked.

"It is a hard life but a good life," said Todor in hesitant but competent English, the *lingua franca* of the world at large, Europe in general and the van in particular. "But I have debts."

He glanced back through the rear window of the camper van (dislodging some of the many tomatoes stacked up around him that he'd insisted they bring along). Michael suspected those debts were never going to be repaid.

"So, we will become rich and famous with our Eurovision song like *Poli Genova*."

"Poli...?"

"*Love is a Crime*," said Aisling from the front. "Bulgarian Eurovision entry 2016. Placed fourth."

"Yes. She graduated from Lubomir Pipkov music school like myself. But, Mr Michael, Eurovision is not on until next year. Why are you starting this project now?"

Michael sighed. "I have to save Europe; save the European Union."

"I did not realise it was in danger."

"The UK has voted to leave."

"Oh, that. Very silly. Tomato?"

"Um, no thank you."

"They are good."

"I'll take one," said Heinz.

"Aye, chuck one up here," said Aisling. "And can someone roll me a fat one while they're at it?"

"The thing I do not understand," said Todor, "is why UK wants to leave Europe." He bit into a tomato, getting juices and seeds in his brush-like moustache. "Why would they leave?"

"Some of us wonder the same," said Michael. "They're idiots?"

"No," said Todor.

"No?"

"Just because someone thinks different does not make them an idiot."

"Oh, okay," said Michael. He leaned back (making sure he wasn't leaning on any tomatoes) and thought. "I guess it's, well, it's a bit about immigration. People just think our country is overcrowded."

"They do?" said Todor. "But I have seen pictures. England's green and pleasant land."

"Ah, you know your Blake."

"I know the song. 'And did those feet in ancient times, walk on England's mountains green.'"

"Like feck he did," said Aisling vehemently.

"It would seem unlikely that Our Lord made it as far as Britain during his time on Earth," agreed Michael, who spoke from personal experience, "But, green though it might be, Britain is quite densely populated and people see television images of all these African and Middle Eastern migrants coming over."

"They do know that Africa isn't part of the EU?"

"Oh, they do." He stopped. "Well, I think they do. But they also worry about EU migrants coming over to work. They see a lot of European doctors in our hospitals."

"Taking the jobs of British doctors?"

"Well, no. We don't train enough British doctors to fill those posts. And then there's the EU labourers doing skilled and unskilled jobs. Portuguese fruit-pickers. Polish plumbers."

"Cracking lads," said Aisling. "Work like demons."

"They have that reputation," Michael agreed.

"Which British plumbers do not have?" said Todor, confused.

"I couldn't possibly say. I do know that a lot of young British people wouldn't want to do those unskilled jobs. The fruit-picking, the cleaning, the social care work. They see it as beneath them."

"And this is why they want to leave?"

Michael struggled. "I think it's more elemental than that. People feel that they need to reclaim their own British sovereignty."

"Sovereignty?" said Todor, not understanding the world.

"Those cheeky and contrary Brits want to rule themselves," said Heinz. "They don't want to have their laws written by European politicians."

"They trust their own government more than the European one?" said Todor, nodding understanding.

"Lord, no," said Michael. "They despised David Cameron as a self-serving toffee-nosed Etonian. And Osbourne. And Boris Johnson. I don't think any of them have an ounce of faith in the new Prime Minister."

"But the opposition politicians are popular though, yes?"

"What opposition?" said Michael. "You mean the retired geography teacher running the Labour party? The Liberals who don't have enough MPs to form a football team? Or that small-island fascist who pretends he's no longer the leader of UKIP and is buddying up to Trump in America?"

Todor thought on this, long and hard. "So," he said eventually, "Your people voted to leave EU because they don't want more people in their country, including the doctors who run your hospitals, the people who do the jobs British people do not want to do and those refugees that aren't even coming from the EU. They also would rather be ruled by a bunch of wealthy capitalist pigs – and pig-fuckers—"

"Alleged pig-fucker," Michael said.

"—rather than by the broad range of political parties in Europe."

"Um, yes," said Michael. "But there's also objections to the silly laws that the EU has supposedly imposed on us. You know, things like the banning of bendy bananas, forcing cows to wear nappies, darts being banned in pubs, enforced metrication, mushy peas being outlawed, shandy too, and both Trafalgar Square and

Waterloo station being made to change their names to avoid offending the French."

"I've not heard of any of those laws," said Heinz.

"Of course you haven't," said Michael. "They were all made up by British newspapers."

"Why?"

"To sell newspapers?"

"And the people believed these lies?"

"I really, honestly couldn't say."

"But they voted to leave anyway," said Heinz.

Todor nodded. "I was wrong. You were right."

"About what?" said Michael.

"They're idiots."

They stopped for the night in the foothills of the Carpathian Mountains, which Aisling claimed was well on the way to their next destination: Cluj-Napoca. Michael had seen the map that Aisling was using: it showed Austria-Hungary as a single entity. He'd realised why they hadn't used any motorways so far, and why their journey was taking so long.

"And what's in Cluj-Napoca?" asked Heinz.

"The key to victory," said Michael and wouldn't be drawn further.

They parked in a small wooded glade overlooking a valley. Before it got completely dark it was clear there were stunning views to be had. Michael looked forward to seeing the place in the morning.

"These mountains are one of the few areas in Europe that still has wild wolves," said Todor cheerfully.

"Will we see any?" said Michael, nervously.

"Maybe. If we're lucky."

Michael resolved that they should build a camp fire. He had bought some sleeping bags from a stall on Todor's market. He imagined even in autumn it would be tolerable to sleep in the wilderness if they had a heat source. He wandered the area, gathering dried branches, which he piled up. Heinz had a lighter, and with some cajoling they got the fire lit. They sat around, toasting their feet and Michael felt enormously pleased with himself.

"Isn't this wonderful, bonding over a camp fire?"

Perhaps it was the flickering of the firelight, but it looked for a moment as though Aisling was rolling her eyes.

"So, Mr Tomato-man," said Aisling.

"Me?" said Todor, around a mouthful of red.

"You said you graduated from the Lubomir Pipkov. That's a bloody prestigious school."

"Three years. Voice and piano."

"Sing us something." Aisling said it in such an imperious tone she might as well have said, "Dance for our entertainment, scum! Dance for your supper!"

"Very well," said Todor and whipped out his electronic organ. It was an antediluvian thing which wheezed like an asthmatic grandpa and was held together with black tape. He turned it on and selected a disco beat. And he sang, drawing high pure notes from his manly frame.

"*The snow glows white on the mountain tonight.*

"*Not a footprint to be seen.*"

"If that's *Let It Go*, I will burst someone," said Aisling.

"It might be," said Todor. "You don't approve?"

Aisling gave him a stony look.

"Maybe something less wintry," suggested Michael, hugging himself.

"I know." Todor turned up the tempo and launched into something with a reggae beat and delivered with a reasonably accurate but nonetheless racist Jamaican accent.

"*Under the Sea?*" said Aisling, cutting him dead at the chorus. "Can't you give us something with some gravitas and power?"

"Okay. *Salagadoola mechicka boola. Bibbidi-bo—*"

"No!"

"*Chim chiminy, chim chimi—*"

"No!"

"*Zip-a-dee-doo—*"

"Jesus, Mary and Joseph! *Nothing from a Disney film!*"

And Todor sang again. "*Many nights we prayed...*"

The song began low, building slowly, powerfully and surely in, what Michael realised, was a duet Todor sang with himself. The lyrics were enticingly familiar but Michael couldn't place them. They rose to a virtuoso crescendo and Todor silenced the Bontempi as the final note reverberated across the Romanian mountainside.

The fact Aisling hadn't interrupted Todor's performance or punched anyone told Michael the songsmith was at least a little impressed.

"What was that?" said Heinz.

"*When You Believe* from *Prince of Egypt*," said Todor.

"I said no Disney," said Aisling.

"It is not Disney," said Todor. "Is DreamWorks."

"You know," said Aisling, "I confess I had my doubts about Michael's selection methods, but I'm thinking you'll shape up just grand. Now, I wonder if you'll try out this song I've written. It's about figs but, like all the best songs, its meaning is multi-layered."

"You know," said Michael, "I might get some of those pine branches. They will add a pleasant fragrance to the fire."

He headed off into the trees to get some distance from Aisling's fig-obsession. He remembered where he'd seen some pine branches, although it was now too dark to see clearly. He felt around for a good five minutes and picked a couple up, before heading back towards the light of the fire.

A huge shape lumbered in front of him, blotting out the fire. It made a low guttural sound and Michael dropped the branches in fright. This thing was too big to be a wolf. Oh, fuck! he thought. It's a bear! Had Todor said anything about bears?

Michael tried to remember anything he'd heard about surviving an encounter with a wild bear. Wasn't there something about making a lot of noise? He opened his mouth and bellowed the first thing that came into his head, in a panicky shriek.

"*Fig tree, my lovely fig tree.*

"*Nobody could ever accuse you of bigotry.*"

The shape in front of him laughed heartily. It moved forward to slap him on the shoulder. "Excellent song, my friend," said Todor. "Came to see if you wanted a tomato."

3rd November 2016

Cluj-Napoca, Romania

The next day's drive to Cluj-Napoca was punctuated with tomato breaks. By the time they pulled up outside the Gheorghe Dima Music Academy in the late morning, Michael was keen to find alternative foodstuffs at any cost. They all stopped to take in the futuristic spectacle of the building. Michael thought it looked like a giant sandwich toaster but realised he was probably just hungry. They walked into reception and headed for the canteen.

"*Unde te duci*?" asked a woman at the reception desk.

"We were just going to grab a bite to eat," replied Michael in his impeccable Romanian.

"Are you students at the academy?"

"No," said Michael, "but—"

"The canteen is only for students. I'm afraid you can't come in."

"Well, I have come to borrow something from your Musical History Department. Could you please tell me where I might find it?"

"You have an appointment?"

Michael didn't get the chance to respond. Heinz leapt forward and gathered the woman's hands in his own. "Iliana, can it really be you?"

Her mouth dropped open in response and she stuttered briefly, lost for words.

Heinz turned to the others and explained. "Iliana and I lived in a commune many years ago. She was one of my earliest muses. When I started to do the nude photos she was always there. Oh the light and shade of her supple body remains with me even now! Some of my favourite pictures from my first portfolio are here on my phone. Shall I show you?"

She slammed her palm down onto the desk, her face scarlet. "Heinz, I have moved on from that part of my life! I must ask you not to share or display those images if you please. It would cause me a good deal of distress."

Heinz pouted. "Art belongs to everyone, Iliana, you always believed that." He started to scroll through images on his phone.

"I believed in a lot of crazy ideas back then, Heinz. The inner goodness of my fellow men, the healing power of crystals, the idea you couldn't contract venereal diseases if you did it standing up. I was wrong about a lot of things." She hissed at Michael. "What is it you need?"

"Sorry?" said Michael, whose brain had become stuck at "venereal diseases".

"Quickly now. What did you want to borrow from the Musical History Department? I will see what I can do and then you will take this man away as quickly as you possibly can. Deal?"

Michael nodded. "Of course. It's the Lucky Eurovision Gibson SG."

Aisling gasped. "The Lucky Eurovision Gibson SG!"

Todor played a "shock horror" *dun dun dunnn!* on his keyboard.

"But it's a myth!" said Heinz. "The guitar which won six Eurovisions."

"Not a myth," said Aisling. "But it was lost."

"Not lost. Stolen," said Michael, "Leading to Romania's disqualification from this year's competition."

"You must keep your voices down!" urged the receptionist. "Now, please step over there and wait. I insist Heinz puts his phone away or I will not make the call."

A few minutes later a pale blonde girl struggled downstairs, carrying a huge case. She walked up to Iliana and whispered to her, before leaving the case and returning upstairs, scowling over her shoulder.

Iliana coughed delicately and indicated the lengthy case, which could only have held a guitar if someone had sawed the instrument into plank-sized segments and laid them end to end. "This will have to do. I am afraid it is not the Lucky Eurovision guitar."

"But the Lucky Eurovision Gibson SG—" said Michael.

"—has been transferred to a secure vault in the presidential palace and access will not be possible at this time. This however is

58

an instrument of remarkable provenance. Are you familiar with the bucium?"

Michael shook his head.

"It is an ancient instrument used by shepherds for communication."

Michael frowned. He would rather have something tuneful. This sounded like a primitive foghorn.

Iliana continued. "There are some very famous frescoes at the monastery of Voroneţ, showing the bucium being played by an angel."

"Really?" Michael thought for a moment. How many times had Gabriel subjected all of the archangels to those insufferable recitals on his blasted horn? If there were musical exams for playing a biblical ram's horn, Gabriel wouldn't have made it past grade one. Never stopped him playing his own tuneless version of any song which took his fancy, though. It had reached the point where Michael couldn't even listen to *Once in Royal David's City*. It would be quite nice to indulge in a little bit of revenge horn.

The guitar had been on Michael's list because of its extraordinary run of success in previous Eurovision song contests. However, he did his best to convince the others the bucium would bring them unspecified kudos and success.

"A mountain horn?" said Aisling. "Hardly rock and roll, is it?"

"Well, I expect Eurovision's finest songwriter will be able to accommodate it," said Michael smoothly.

"Or use it as a massive hash pipe," mused Heinz.

Budapest was an architectural spectacle, and as Aisling drove through the city, they all stared out of the windows at the grand Art Nouveau and neo-classical buildings in the fading light of the early evening.

"If you really want theme that means something to Europe, how about the Danube?" suggested Todor as they drove across the river via the huge Chain Bridge. "It goes through many countries in the EU."

Michael tapped his tablet. "Nine countries; astonishing! That is a very interesting idea, Todor."

Aisling muttered.

"What was that Aisling?" asked Michael. "Do you have some ideas already?"

"No, I was just reflecting nothing rhymes with Danube," she said. "It's a non-starter for a song. Why do you think Strauss wrote instrumentals?"

Michael wanted to reply nineteenth century waltzes were invariably instrumentals, and that *The Blue Danube* was no exception, but Heinz interjected.

"Lube!"

"What?" said Michael.

"Lube rhymes with Danube! Surely we can make it work?"

Michael's face fell. He could instantly see where this might end up. "I'm not—"

"So it does!" said Aisling gleefully. "And pube, now you mention it. Let's think. It might go something like this." She swayed and crooned.

"I'm like a boat upon the Danube

"I slip right in—"

"No!" howled Michael. "We simply can't have *rudeness* like that!"

"There's a rich history of rudeness in Eurovision," Heinz pointed out. "Bucks Fizz won when they whipped off the girls' skirts, didn't they?"

"I would categorise that as *sauciness*" said Michael. "There could definitely be a place for sauciness in our act, but not *rudeness*. I must draw the line at lube and pube."

"Boob!" shouted Heinz.

Aisling laughed raucously.

Heinz leaned forward, suddenly animated. "This is good news! I think we agree upon some things here. A saucy video is the way to go, for sure."

"I think I'm way ahead of you, Heinz," said Michael in a tired voice. "By saucy, you mean naked don't you?"

"No," said Heinz, triumphant. "My idea is much, much smarter than that. We should be naked and have—"

"So we are all naked, then."

"Well, we are all naked, underneath our clothes, aren't we? But I was going to say we have wearable tech covering our bodies, all projecting amazing, co-ordinated images."

Surprisingly, Michael found himself taken with Heinz's idea. It had the potential to create a real spectacle. "Hmm, I wonder where we can get wearable tech, at short notice," he mused. "It's not all that commonplace at the moment."

"I have some very creative ideas, Michael," said Heinz. "Leave it with me."

"As long as there can also be doves?" came Todor's voice.

"What?"

"Doves. And dry ice."

"Isn't that all a bit cheesy?"

"If I can be in video with doves and dry ice, I can die a happy man!"

"Right so," announced Aisling. "The Hungarian State Opera House,"

They craned forward to look as she brought the van to a stop, pulling on the handbrake with a loud screech. A doorman approached. Aisling tried to wind down the window; when the winder came away in her hand, she opened the door instead.

"*On nem parkolhatnak itt*," said the doorman.

"We're picking someone up," said Michael.

The doorman regarded the wretched campervan with an unconcealed sneer. "Very well, sir. The opera house would be *delighted* if you were able to move on within five minutes, to permit other vehicles to use the space."

Aisling closed the door and turned to the others. "What now? I get the distinct feeling we're not dressed for the opera. Michael, you know who we're here for, shall we get your man there to pass on a message?"

Michael looked down at himself in dismay. Ordinarily, he would be immaculately dressed, but three days' travelling, combined with last night's rough camping experience in the Carpathian mountains had left him grubby, stained, and perhaps a little bit smelly.

"Her name is Ibolya Zsengellar and she's an opera singer," said Michael. "She also had a minor pop hit in the Eighties with the song, *Bang Bang my Boom Boom*. I can hardly see her coming out to the pavement just because someone sends a message. She will need some persuading, and I'm not sure how we can do it, dressed as we all are."

"I will do it, no problem," said Todor.

"You can't do it, you're dressed like— What is it you're dressed like, exactly?" asked Michael.

"A colourful peasant," said Heinz.

"Maybe one of the chorus from Tchaikovsky's *Eugene Onegin*," said Todor with a wink. Before anyone could object, the sliding door was open and he had slipped out.

"Meet us in the nearest café on the main road," called Michael.

Aisling started the engine. They watched as the huge man lumbered around to the stage door and disappeared from view.

Michael, Aisling and Heinz passed two hours in the café discussing Todor's possible fate. Michael visited the toilets and attempted to spruce up his appearance slightly with damp paper towels, hoping he appeared careless and bohemian. Knowing, deep inside, he looked like a tramp who'd simply wiped his face.

"I bet he's been thrown out," said Aisling.

"No, a resourceful guy like that will be fine," insisted Heinz. "I would not be surprised if he is in the orchestra pit by now, enhancing the ensemble with his Bontempi."

At that moment the café door opened and Todor walked in with a statuesque woman. She was dressed in an outfit which reminded Michael of a fortune teller's tent. Todor had somehow acquired a gold cape. He twirled it flamboyantly as they approached the table.

"Best party ever," said Todor.

"Such naïve charm," said the statuesque woman.

"Ibolya Zsengellar, everyone," said Todor.

"Charmed," said Heinz and kissed her hand.

"Ibolya is a megastar," said Todor, speaking like a sudden convert, "but she will come with us because of the excellent company."

The woman gave him a twinkling smile.

Michael pulled out a chair for Ibolya to sit down. "You know about out music project?" he asked her.

"It is fine. I explained," said Todor.

Ibolya addressed the group. She actually addressed the entire café, as her voice had a penetrating quality, like a great orator. Or a drill. "I had just come off stage. I am currently performing the role of Grandmother Burya in *Jenůfa*, you see. Happily, it is a role where I can relax early in the evening, so I spent some time understanding your fascinating mission from this accomplished gentleman."

"We had champagne!" said Todor, giddily.

"We certainly did!" boomed Ibolya. "We drank champagne from France, and we ate the finest pastries from Austria. All of this is possible through a strong and united Europe. I am committed to keeping it together in any way I can. I am a member of the European parliament, as well as being a singer, did you know this?"

"It was mentioned in our dossier," said Michael.

"A dossier! How clandestine!" Yes, I am the only politician in Brussel who can shatter a wine glass with her voice! Who wants to see that?" She swept an arm round the entire café, inviting everyone's opinion.

"How much champagne has she drunk, would you say?" Michael asked Todor, *sotto voce.*

Todor started to count on his fingers but gave up and shrugged. "I've lost count," he said. "But I've had a bit too, so..."

"Hey, Ibolya, can I teach you a song about figs?" said Aisling, leaping to her feet. "It's got some real tricky parts. I haven't been able to properly master it myself."

Aisling and Ibolya went into an intense, not all together silent huddle. Michael stepped away from the group to pay the bill and enquire about somewhere they might get rooms for the night. Perhaps with good sound insulation. He checked his cards and found that one was missing. He was just about to call up the bank's app to report the card lost or stolen when his phone vibrated. He answered.

"Hello, Mr Michaels? It's Trish from *A Song For Europe.*"

"You're from the BBC?" said Michael. "I'm pretty excited about next year's Eurovision. I can tell you we're going to blow—"

"Yes, we've got your application form here. We don't need too many details from you now, Mr Michaels. That can all come later. It's just a courtesy call to say that your form was successfully submitted."

"That's wonderful."

"There is just one small detail I need to clarify with you, though. You haven't told us the name of your act."

"The act?"

"I can add that to the record, if you'd like to give it to me."

"Well, I'm still in the process of forming it. If you could see us now. Honestly!" He looked at his party. An Irishwoman, a Finn, a Bulgarian youth and now an operatic Hungarian eurocrat. "It's all the countries of the world, or it certainly feels like it. Hello...? Hello—!"

The battery had died. Never mind. Michael checked his watch, wondering if there might be anywhere still open selling coloured chinos. Ibolya hit a high note in the fig song and a wineglass shattered on the other side of the café.

Concord, North Carolina

Clovenhoof's eight hundred mile journey to North Carolina could briefly be described as beaches and palm trees, followed by rivers and mossy woodland, followed by shaggy forests. All of it interspersed with low-rise housing, isolated fast food outlets and the rusting shells of defunct factories and businesses. Clovenhoof and Mason ate breakfast cheeseburgers at Whataburger in mid-Florida and a Chicken Finger Plate lunch at a Zaxby's in South Carolina. None of it had an impact on Clovenhoof's constipated innards, and he listened to the lullaby of his churning guts as Mason drove the last couple of hundred miles: up round Charlotte and out to an entertainment arena in the suburb of Concord.

By the time Mason found a space in the nearly full parking lot, evening had fallen.

"I'll be waiting here when you're done, bro," said Mason, pulling his flat cap over his eyes and sliding down his chair to sleep.

"And if you forget where we parked, just remember, mine's the only vehicle that isn't a pick-up with raised suspension."

Clovenhoof climbed out, carrying his weapon of choice, and strode into the arena. It was an odd building, with all the charm of a down-at-heel dog-racing track. It couldn't decide if it was a warehouse, a sports stadium or an oversized village hall. From the already busy floor, rows of plastic seating rose up in tiers to the corrugated iron wall. Flags, pro-Trump banners and harsh spotlights hung from the rafters. Placards aplenty and TV crews were in attendance. Many supporters waved *Women for Trump* cards. Some waved unofficial *It's time to grab America by the pussy!* cards.

A middle-aged woman in a glittering red cowboy hat stopped Clovenhoof. "And what do you have here?" she cooed.

"Patriotic brownies," said Clovenhoof. He'd stuck a little flag on a cocktail stick in the central one.

"Well, aren't they just darling?" she said.

"Please," he said, proffering the tray.

"Not for me, sweetheart. I'm watching my weight but – Gill! Gill! Come over here and try one of these."

A man in a baseball cap and several acres of checked shirt, who was clearly not watching his weight, came ambling through with several friends in tow.

"Wha' is it, Paislee?" he said.

"You must try this darling man's brownies."

"Where they at?" said Gill, scooping up one of the LSD-laced cakes.

"Pass them round," suggested Clovenhoof. The tray was lifted away and absorbed into the crowd. Job done. The way Clovenhoof reasoned it, if Trump supporters were clueless bigots most of the time anyway then a light dosing of hallucinogenic narcotics would tip them over into full blown loons.

"You're not from round here, are you?" said Paislee.

"How can you tell?" Clovenhoof gave a raffish grin.

"You got one of them posh accents, like him on *House*. You here to cause trouble?"

"Oh, I cause trouble everywhere," he said.

Paislee laughed. "Well, a word in your ear. It don't matter how posh you talk, the boys round here don't take kindly to liberals. There was a girl up there, with a big Jew star on her coat, making some protests about something. And a man with a sign – something about the Nazis. Security had them out of here before the boys could give them the kicking of their lives."

"Duly noted," said Clovenhoof. "And your opinion on liberals, Paislee?"

"Oh, I haven't got time for their nonsense either," she said, amiably enough. "They're like the speech police. Tell us what we can and can't say. I thought we had freedom of speech. Time was when I could call a black a black. I could call a homosexual a homosexual. Time was when men went in the men's restroom and women went in the women's restroom. And now, apparently, any man in a dress can whip his wangdoodle out wherever he likes. There's so much political correctness 'bout what I can and can't say I don't know if I'm coming or going." She wrinkled her nose unhappily. "Liberals. With their trigger warnings and their safe spaces. What the hell is a safe space anyhow?"

"I genuinely do not know," said Clovenhoof.

"That's what I like about Trump," said Paislee. "He calls a spade a spade. He speaks his mind. He isn't afraid to speak the truth and point out what's wrong with this country."

"And what's that?"

Paislee gave him a meaningful look. "All the damn illegal aliens and terrorists," she said simply. "Mexicans stealing our jobs. Syrian refugees coming over here and bringing their Al Qaeda terrorism with them."

"The refugees are all terrorists?"

"Not all of them, but it's like that bowl of Skittles." Clovenhoof had no idea what bowl she was on about. "If there's a bowl of Skittles, a hundred Skittles in a bowl, and you knew one of those Skittles was poisoned, would you eat them?"

"What is life without a little risk?" said Clovenhoof.

"No, sweetheart. You throw them Skittles out. Trump's gonna build that wall and make the Mexicans pay for it. What's Obama doing? He's letting them hide out in sanctuary cities. He's letting them get away with murder and robbery. You see, folks over in

Washington, they're obsessed with helping the illegal aliens and homosexuals in dresses. They keep saying black lives matter. Well, what about white lives? Washington doesn't care about us. Trump does. He believes in this country. One nation, under God. Under God! Obama, that liar Clinton and all of Washington has forgotten this is a Christian country with Christian morals. If Jesus could vote, he'd vote for Trump."

"I wasn't aware Mr Trump was a Christian."

"He's a winner, that's what he is!" said Paislee passionately. "He's living the American dream. He builds things. He fights. He wins. America loves a winner. And Jesus loves a winner too."

Clovenhoof, who had met Jesus during his gap years on Earth, found this doubtful. Jesus' greatest trick, in Clovenhoof's opinion, wasn't turning water into wine or bringing Lazarus back from the dead; it was turning an obvious failure into a PR victory. Getting nailed by the Romans was a pretty clear cut sign of a loser but, to hear the bloody Church go on about it, it was apparently the most cunning and resounding of victories.

Maybe Trump was like Jesus. Maybe you could polish a turd.

An hour after Trump left the arena stage to wild applause and more than a couple of "Yeehaws!" Clovenhoof trudged out to the parking lot. The North Carolina night was still and balmy. Clovenhoof kicked the headlights in on every alternative car on his way to Mason's taxicab, but it did nothing to raise his mood.

The car alarms he set off were enough to wake Mason. He sniffled, sat up and groaned. "Job done?" he asked as Clovenhoof got in.

"'Job done?'" sneered Clovenhoof in a very squeaky and very sarcastic voice. "This is a country full of morons."

"Watch your mouth, bro," said Mason, though without much rancour. "You can say it's a state full of morons, fine. But this is my country. We invented the lightbulb, the airplane and the nuclear bomb and we've got a one hundred percent record in winning world wars so just watch your mouth."

"Country full of morons," repeated Clovenhoof sullenly.

Mason punched him in the shoulder: hard, but like it was for his own good. "What's the problem?"

Clovenhoof produced his phone and scrolled through his snippets of video. "I gave out over fifty acid brownies. The TV news crews were doing live vox pop segments before and after the rally. I was there. I filmed them." He angled the phone round for Mason to see and pressed play.

A woman, talking to camera: "Hillary has too many hormones. She could start a war in ten seconds."

Cut to a skinny man who looked like he'd been on the all-bourbon diet: "Hillary has a body double who goes out and does all her public appearances."

"Why?" asked the news reporter. "Why would she do that?"

"Because she's dying," said the skinny man. "She's got dementia from all that cocaine she's been doing."

Cut to a young woman in an oversized T-shirt: "I mean she's a lesbian. Everyone knows that. Hillary's in love with Huma Abedin. That marriage to Bill is a sham. That's why Huma Abedin left that wiener of a husband. It's gonna be Madam President and the First Lady."

Cut to a red-faced guy with bulging frog-eyes. "And that's why Canadians are refusing to sell us any more bacon."

"Because...?" prompted the reporter.

"Trump is going to use it as part of his extreme vetting. You wanna come through our wall? You wanna come into our country? Eat this bacon. Eat it. Show that you're not one of them ISIS terrorists. They can't eat bacon. They can't do it. And that's why they're poisoning the bacon."

"Who is poisoning the bacon? Canada?"

"No, man!" said frog-eyes. "ISIS. ISIS are poisoning our bacon. You tried to buy any in Walmart lately, have you? No, you haven't. ISIS are poisoning our bacon."

Cut to a sweet, curly-haired granny: "Cos Trump's got to stop Obama. We've got to have that wall because Obama wants to make us all into one big country. Mexico down there and Canada up there. That's what that NAFTA thing is about. He wants to sell us out. He wants to flood the country with Mexicans cos they're going to vote for him."

Cut to a man in a thin beard and sunglasses: "Door to door gun confiscation. They've got a secret code word and one day

Obama is gonna pick up the phone and say that code word and that's the signal. Every law enforcement agency in the land, with no warning, will go from house to house, taking folks' guns. From my cold dead hand, Obama!"

Cut to a big guy with a bead of spit at the corner of his mouth: "Chemtrails," he said as though nothing else needed to be said.

"What about them?" said an off-camera voice.

"President Trump will stop the chemtrails. All those planes, going back and forth. Don't tell me that's water vapour coming off their wings. I ain't dumb. Chemtrails. And you know why they're doing it? It's the atheists, trying to kill off the angels in heaven. I seen the evidence. Don't tell me it ain't happening."

Cut to a woman in a smart suit, as though she'd come straight from the office or the bank: "And we're still not getting answers about Hillary Clinton's e-mail server. She's under investigation by the FBI. They're going to find those e-mails and they will prove she had all those people killed. Vince Foster, Ron Brown. She killed Kathleen Willey's cat. She did."

Cut to a young man who seemed too excited to control his own breathing, let alone his speech: "Hillary is a *demon*. She *is* a demon. Everyone knows it. Even Donald Trump – God bless Donald Trump! – knows it but he can't say it or else the Washington media will ... will— He can't say it. She is the spawn of hell and she has been sent to torment us."

Cut to a pair of near-identical men in Blue Devils basketball shirts: "And what are we gonna call her? What is it? Presidentess?"

"Presidentess," said the other.

"And what about the oval office?"

"They're gonna have to change it round cos she's a woman."

"Yeah, they're gonna have to change it because she's a woman."

Cut to a grey-bearded man who simply shouted: "Fluoride! Fucking fluoride in the water! They been doing it for decades and no one's stopping them! They're not getting me! I've been drinking my own water for years! My own fucking water! Someone better do something about it, you hear me, or there's gonna be a reckoning. My own fucking water! Jesus!"

Cut to a woman who looked like a mad old cat lady who'd just lost all her cats in a court hearing: "You can feel it, can't you?" she whispered to camera. "And you know it's happening. Barack *Hussein* Obama. Huma *Mahmood* Abedin. People say that this place is going to turn into the Islamic States of America. No. No. It's already happened. They're everywhere. It's already happened. They're watching us now. Watching!"

Clovenhoof stopped the video and stared at Mason.

"I'd say they were pretty spectacular results," said the taxi driver.

"Yeah?" said Clovenhoof. "So you'd be able to tell me which ones were on acid and which were clean and sober morons?"

"They weren't all high?"

"Nope," said Clovenhoof.

Mason was thoughtful. "Show me again."

Clovenhoof did.

"Okay. That one's on acid," said Mason.

"No."

"That one?"

"No."

"He is."

"Is not."

"What? Mr 'ISIS poison our bacon'?"

"Wide awake and all cylinders firing."

"Okay. But that one?"

"Nope. The guy dribbling into his cup behind her is. But she didn't eat one."

"The chemtrails guy was on acid though, surely?"

"He had a brownie, yep."

"See?"

"But he was saving it for later."

"Jeez."

Mason watched through all the clips a second time, even went back to some of them a third time. In the end, working out which opinions were drug-inspired and which were just bat-shit stupid was nothing more than guesswork.

"It's chemically impossible to make Trump supporters come across as any more stupid than they already are," said Clovenhoof, frustrated.

"I could have told you that," said Mason. "One of the beauties of this country. You think you're scraping the bottom of the barrel. That barrel has no bottom, bro."

Clovenhoof shook his head and consulted his three part plan to defeat plan. His first strand had failed utterly. There was no discrediting the man or his followers. He was Teflon and they were rubber. No filth would stick to the man himself and his supporters repelled any assault with a shield of idiocy.

"I've got to convince him to step down," Clovenhoof decided.

"Good luck with that," snorted Mason.

"He's already left here but he's appearing in Reno on Saturday night. I'll speak to him then."

"If you say so."

Clovenhoof patted Mason. "To Reno, my good chap."

Mason looked at him like he was crazy and laughed. "You any idea how far Reno is from here, bro?"

"No. That's why I've got you, Tonto."

"I am not driving you to Reno. You need to catch a plane."

"You're losing a fare here, Mason."

Mason started the engine. "I'm driving to a Motel 6. We're booking two rooms. I'm gonna sleep for twelve hours straight. And then I will drop you off at Charlotte Douglas airport and go home."

"I thought we were in this together, Mason. Like Bonnie and Clyde, Butch Cassidy and the Sundance Kid. Like Bert and Ernie."

"Motel 6," said Mason firmly. "And you'd better have the cash to pay."

4th November 2016

Budapest, Hungary

Michael woke up in high spirits. A night in a comfy bed, even though he'd shared the family room with Heinz, Aisling and Todor, had restored him greatly.

Todor's bed was empty. It was probably in the blood of the green grocer to be an early riser.

Michael went out and bought fresh fruit and some *kifli* yeast rolls so that they could get on the road straightaway, but everyone was slow to rise. Ibolya's room was so quiet, Michael wondered if she'd gone out for a walk. Eventually she opened the door, a hotel sheet wrapped around her. Her makeup had slid down her face like a selection of wax crayons left on top of a hot radiator. She sank to her knees after the effort of standing upright proved too much and looked at Michael with a deeply pained expression.

"Please don't make so much noise," she begged.

"I haven't spoken. Did you go straight to bed last night?" asked Michael, realisation dawning.

"Yes! We went straight to bed after the party," said Ibolya.

"Party? What party?" asked Michael.

"The end of the *Jenůfa* run party," said Ibolya. "It's a tradition and I couldn't miss it! We went after you left us. Todor found it *such* an education."

"I bet he did." Michael surveyed the wrecked room. "Right, I'll get you some orange juice, and paracetamol if you need it. We should be on the road to Switzerland."

"Soon, yes. Maybe noon, or a little after?" offered Ibolya.

"No," said Michael firmly. "We need to leave within the next thirty minutes."

"Don't worry." Todor's muffled voice came from under one of the pillows on Ibolya's huge and ruffled bed. "I have a plan. When this is all over we tie him in a chair and you sing at him until his eyeballs pop."

"That's the spirit! Up you get!" said Michael cheerily, and pulled the door shut behind him.

Hours later, they were driving through Austria, the sun high in the sky over emerald fields and the blue of a distant lake.

"Can you hear that noise, Aisling?" Michael said, frowning.

"Which one? The rustling of the tomato sacks, the snoring of the hungover diva, or the sound of Heinz farting and trying to cover it up with a cough?"

"Hey!" protested Heinz.

"No, listen. It's more like a knocking sound. Almost as if it could be the engine, but it's coming from the back," said Michael.

Aisling gave him a withering look, but before either of them could speak there was a loud bang from the back. The van shuddered to an abrupt halt.

"Well that's strange," said Michael. "Something's definitely gone at the back, but what's happened to the engine? Why don't you open the bonnet and we'll take a look?"

Aisling pointed at the front of the vehicle. "Michael, do you see where our legs are?"

"Yes," said Michael, hesitantly.

"And do you see how close to the outside they are?"

"Ye–es."

"The engine *is* in the back, yer feckin', half-boiled eejit!"

Michael turned in his seat; he shouted in horror. Flames were licking up the rear of the van, presumably from the now defunct engine. "Out everyone! Quickly!"

The entire band – even the snoring Ibolya – went from nought to total evacuation in under ten seconds. They stood by the side of the road as Aisling tackled the fire with a tiny extinguisher she'd grabbed from under her seat. It was very clear the extinguisher was never going to quench the fire's enthusiasm until it had done a lot more damage. Eventually Aisling threw it down in disgust.

"What do we do now?" she said.

Michael pointed. "There's a town up ahead. Let's see if we can get help."

After half a mile, they reached a car park next to a lake. Apart from a parked up coach, the car park was empty. The town was another half mile or so distant.

74

"Hold my bag for a tick," said Heinz. "I will see if there's someone on the bus who can help us

Michael smiled confidently at the group as they waited. "I know this seems like a setback, but you can be sure we'll be back on the road in no time at all."

"Some of us didn't want to be on the road at this ungodly hour," muttered Ibolya.

There was a toot from behind. Michael turned to see that the coach had pulled up, and Heinz was at the wheel.

"Hop on everyone, we got transport!"

They climbed on board. Michael nodded a greeting to the small band of elderly passengers, mostly American, who were already on the bus, and took a seat behind Heinz. The others found seats further back.

"Why are you driving the coach?" Michael hissed.

"*The Sound of Music* tour!" Heinz replied. "Their driver is on a break, so I'm taking over. I can't find a hat to wear, sadly."

"*The Sound of Music*? Are you serious?"

"This is Austria, my friend."

A growing sense of excitement gripped Michael. He peered through the windscreen. "So, we're touring the locations where the movie was shot? And we're presently in—"

Heinz thrust a colourful guide booklet at him but Michael was already tippy-tappy-typing on his tablet.

"We're in Mondsee!" he squealed.

"Oh. Okay," said Heinz.

"If we drive up here a little way we come to the church where Maria and Georg were married."

"Who?"

"This is wonderful!" Michael noticed that there was a microphone at the front of the coach. He picked it up, flicking it on and turning to address the passengers. "We're delighted to join you on today's tour. I'm not sure if you've had a chance to sing the classic melodies from *Sound of Music* yet, but we have some very special guests on the coach to help things along. Shall we start with *My Favourite Things*?"

"Huh," said Todor sourly. "They do not like Disney but Rogers and Hammerstein is all hunky dunky."

The church at Mondsee, its yellow and white exterior so gay and bright in the late autumn sun, was utterly charming. Ibolya was much in demand for photos after delivering an ear-splitting rendition of *Climb Ev'ry Mountain* on the coach.

Michael spent his time there just standing by the church entrance, hands clasped, thinking about the glorious wedding scene from the movie. The story of Maria, forced from her religious role in life and finding herself in a loving relationship that no-one expected, was one Michael felt closely echoed his own. True, his beloved Andy wasn't an Austro-Hungarian naval captain and it was deeply unlikely that Andy had a tiny army of von Trapp children for Michael to adopt, but otherwise it was a close fit.

"I don't get it," said a voice.

Michael looked round. "What don't you get?" he asked the American teenager.

"What everyone's excited about."

"It's the film, *The Sound of Music,*" said Michael. "You must have seen it?"

He shook his head.

"It's sublime!" gushed Michael. "It's got everything a story should have. A wholesome leading lady, a delightful love story, and a family's flight from the evil of the Nazis."

"What's a Nazi?"

"What's a— Surely you're not serious?"

The teen shrugged.

"You've heard of Hitler? The bad guy who started World War Two? Killed six million Jews? Had a massive army who wore jack boots and marched around doing this?" Michael goose-stepped around the courtyard.

"That just looks dumb," said the teen.

"You must know. All those rallies and everyone going *Heil Hitler.*"

"You mean Hail Hydra?"

"What? No!" Michael held his arm up in a Nazi salute. "*Heil Hitler. Heil Hitler.*"

"Oh," said the boy, slowly understanding. "Like the bad guys from Indiana Jones."

"Yes. Probably."

"What is going on, sir?" said a voice behind Michael.

He whirled, arm still raised, to see two officers in the peaked caps of the *Bundespolizei*. One had his hand casually resting on his pistol holster.

"Hello?" said Michael. "Can I help you?"

"We've been watching you," said one.

"Yes?"

"You are aware that such activity is banned under the Anti-Nazi Prohibition Act."

"What? This?" said Michael, pointing at his still raised arm. "I was just showing the young man."

"And chanting Heil Hitler. We heard."

The other officer dragged Michael's arm down and handcuffed him, before propelling him towards the waiting car.

Charlotte, North Carolina

Clovenhoof sprawled out in the executive lounge at Charlotte Douglas airport and sipped his third piña colada of the day. Clovenhoof had never been in an executive lounge before. It was fine enough, but he quickly understood that the main perk of being in an executive lounge was that you weren't in the bog standard hell of the main airport. To get true enjoyment out of the executive lounge, Clovenhoof had to pop out every few minutes, gaze upon the queues, noise and uncomfortable seating of the airport departure lounge and engage random passers-by in conversation; during which he would casually mention that he was relaxing in the executive lounge, so much nicer than the soulless human conveyer belt out here. It worked really well if he started the conversation with tacit hints that he might invite his travel-weary victim to join him in the cosy and luxurious sanctuary of the lounge. Which, of course, he didn't.

There was one other person in the executive lounge. A blonde woman in a patterned dress sat in the corner furthest from the bar, reading a magazine. Clovenhoof picked up his cocktail and clip-clopped over to the woman. "This is amazing, isn't it?" he said.

"Is it?" said the woman politely.

"When we get on the plane I'm going to sit in the economy class and, when someone says I'm sitting in their seat, I'm going to reply loudly, 'Oh, yes. I forgot! I am in first class!' Then make a real fuss as I go find my seat."

"Why?" said the woman. "Everyone will just think you're some kind of asshole."

"I *am* some kind of asshole," he said as though she had hit upon a great profundity.

There was something familiar about the woman, a playfulness in her expression. He clicked his fingers as he remembered. "You're that singer."

"Maybe," she said.

"I like your song."

"Which one?"

"The one that goes *mmm-cha, mmm-cha, mmm-cha*. You know the one?"

"You don't know the title?"

"I listen to music with my hips, not my ears."

"Good for you," she said, trying to return to her magazine.

"I'm going to Reno," said Clovenhoof, undeterred by someone deliberately ignoring him.

"Uh-huh."

"Where are you going?"

"Cleveland. That's in the opposite direction," she said, pointedly.

"Are you doing a concert there?"

"Kind of."

Clovenhoof recalled a list of dates and venues from his recent research. "You doing a thing with Hillary Clinton?"

She looked at him. She wasn't exactly alarmed, but there was a concerned look in her eyes as she tried to gauge his own political leanings. "Yes. Me and Katy Perry and I can't remember who else. Showing our support for Hillary."

"I've never met Hillary, but I'm sure she's lovely. You know what I really admire about her?"

"What's that?"

"For a grandmother, she seems really good with e-mail."

The singer tried to suppress a smile.

"I saw her on stage the other night," said Clovenhoof. "She was with Bouncy and Jay Zed."

"Jay Z," said the singer.

"It's pronounced *zed*," said Clovenhoof indulgently. "I'm surprised. I wouldn't have thought Hillary would be into that kind of music."

"*That* kind of music? What kind of music do you think the future president should be into?"

"I don't know. Grandma music. Elvis or something. It's just she does seem to get a lot of pop singers up on stage with her. Trump doesn't."

The singer smiled. "You think there are any who'd be willing to share a platform with him?"

Clovenhoof shrugged. "Maybe he doesn't need them. Maybe he's got a personality big enough to fill a stage all by himself."

The singer pulled an expression that said a lot of different things, not many of them necessarily complimentary.

"You don't like him, huh?" he said. "You know, I was at an event last night and there were plenty of people who thought Hillary Clinton was the most evil and scheming woman on earth."

The singer put her magazine down. "No one's perfect," she said.

"I come pretty close," said Clovenhoof.

"This election is like..." She sighed. "Imagine you wanted to go out for dinner. A really special meal at your favourite restaurant. Except your favourite restaurant is closed, so you have two choices. You can go to the Burger King two blocks down and have a Whopper and fries; or you can eat the mouldy, slime-covered thing that's been sat at the back of your refrigerator for the past month. Which do you pick?"

"That's a trick question," said Clovenhoof. He had eaten various slime-covered things and enjoyed most of them.

"It doesn't matter what you dislike about Hillary," said the singer. "The only thing that matters is how horrible the alternative is. And that's why Katy and I are showing our support for her."

"You think she'll sing *I Kissed a Girl and I Liked It*?" asked Clovenhoof.

"Unlikely," said the singer.

"Shame. I really like that song," he said.

"It's a good song."

"I've kissed a girl, and I liked it too."

"It speaks to people on so many levels."

"I've recorded my own version," said Clovenhoof.

"Oh?" said the singer, truly disinterested.

"Yep. *I Kissed a Goat and It Bit Me*."

"I see."

"I've got a video of it on my phone somewhere. I sent it to Michael earlier. It's very entertaining."

The singer, a true professional, gave Clovenhoof a warm and unprejudiced smile. She said, "Show me anything on that phone and I'll call airport security."

Clovenhoof sighed. "You're not the first person to say that to me."

Salzburg, Austria

Michael sat in a cell, reflecting on the turn of fate which had brought him there. He had assembled all of the key components of his Eurovision super group – and in record time! Would they carry on without him? There was no doubt most of them shared his enthusiasm for the project, but none of them knew how high the stakes were. The apocalyptic prophesy could be enabled in a few short days, once America went to the polls.

A police officer came to the cell door and unlocked it. Michael was taken to a side room and given a telephone handset.

"You can make one call," said the officer.

"Only one?" asked Michael, checking his watch. "What if the person I want to call could either be at home or the gym? Can I call both numbers?"

"One call only."

With a heavy sigh, he dialled Clovenhoof's number. Michael was under no illusions about Jeremy's *actual* usefulness, but even he could pass along a message to Andy. He'd get things sorted out.

The call connected.

"Jeremy, I need you to—"

"Yo Mikey, how's it hangin' my friend? That's how we talk here in the executive lounge. Did you check out that video clip I sent you?"

"No."

"I kissed a goat and it bit me,

"The taste of her cud was delicious..."

"Lord, it's worse than the fig song," Michael muttered. "Jeremy!"

"What?"

"I'm a bit limited in what I can do right now, Jeremy, which is why I need you to—"

"Can't stop and talk now, my angelic nemesis, I've got a pop star here who wants a piece of me."

Michael heard a distant, emphatic female voice: "She does *not!*"

"Take care now y'all!" Clovenhoof hung up.

Michael gazed in disbelief at the handset. He looked up at the police officer. "I don't suppose I could—?"

The officer shook his head and led him back to the cell.

Michael was napping on his bunk when the police officer returned. This time he was accompanied by a man with a neat beard, wearing a beautifully cut suit. Michael immediately took a shine to him. You could always trust a man who took tailoring and manscaping seriously.

"Good evening, Mr Michaels," said the man, his English inflected by a playful Austrian accent. "I'm Stefan Grösswang, attorney at law. I need to get your signature on a couple of documents and we can soon have you out of here."

"Out of here."

"To be certain," smiled Stefan.

Michael scribbled his signature and, true to Stefan's word, within an hour he was released. Michael's shoes were returned to him and he sat on the bunk to put them on.

"I hope you will not judge all of Austria based on this experience," said Stefan.

"All a misunderstanding. Many thanks, Herr Grösswang." He offered the man a hearty handshake.

"My pleasure," said Stefan. He nodded a curt farewell but did not move. Michael tied his shoelaces.

Stefan gave a small cough. "I understand from your acquaintances that you are creating a Eurovision act?"

"That is true," said Michael.

"Very admirable."

"And it's essential that I find them all as quickly as possible so we can continue on our mission."

"I wish you the best of luck."

"Thank you."

Stefan turned to leave but still did not go. "I myself have a small amount of talent as a rock guitarist," he said casually.

"Oh?"

"I am in a local band, but they just play covers of classic rock songs."

Michael looked at the lawyer. He was like an eager puppy; a beautifully manscaped puppy. "Perhaps...?"

"I'd love to join you if you have room for another?" said Stefan.

Michael grinned and shook his hand again. "That would be my pleasure, Stefan. Do you have your own guitar?"

Reno, Nevada

"But what do you mean 'declined'?" said Clovenhoof.

The hotel receptionist held up the credit card. "This card," she said, "is no good."

"What do you mean it's no good. It's plenty good. I've used it all over the place with no problem. It's like money."

"Yes, sir," said the receptionist. "But there's no money left on it."

"What?" Clovenhoof snatched the card from her and inspected it closely. "What? Where did it go?"

"I imagine you spent it all, sir."

"Can we put some more on it?" said Clovenhoof and twanged it against the reception counter. "Can't we do that ... contactless thing? You know, *beep*. Contactless. I've seen Michael do it. Can we?"

The receptionist's smile was wearing thin. "What you need to do is phone the credit card company or your bank, sir. And once you've gotten the funds, the Sierra Nevada Hotel and Casino will be happy to book you the room of your choice. But until then—"

Clovenhoof looked at her. "Yes? Until then, what?"

The receptionist made the politest of shooing motions. "You'll have to go someplace else."

"Oh."

Clovenhoof sloped outside onto Virginia Street. At night, the hotels, casinos, shops, pawnbrokers and restaurants of Reno were festooned in an epileptic seizure of illuminations, as though the Almighty Himself had eaten a rainbow and vomited it up on a nowhere desert town. A light breeze worked itself around the night time pedestrians. Clovenhoof turned his collar up and dug through his pockets as he attempted to plan out his next steps.

His pockets were mostly full of sweet wrappers. Apart from the unholy Toblerone bar in his rucksack, he had eaten all his Halloween booty. The effects on his insides had not yet been resolved and he'd considered phoning up the Guinness Book of Records to find out what the record was for the longest period spent on US soil without taking a dump.

Clovenhoof threw away the rubbish from his pockets, letting the wind take it. In doing so he almost lost his last dollar bill. He caught it a split second before it was out of reach and unrolled it. Ten dollars.

"In God We Trust," he read and blew out his lips dismissively. "Learn a little self-reliance, America."

He had ten dollars and a little under twenty-four hours before he could make another attempt to derail Trump's presidency. Ten dollars could buy a hot meal. It might not get him a hotel room, but it should find him somewhere he could have a shower, a shave and generally spruce himself up. If these were his last funds, he needed to spend them wisely.

There was a casino across the street.

5th November 2016

Salzburg, Austria

Stefan Grösswang, attorney at law and enthusiastic guitarist, reunited Michael with the others, who were all staying in a youth hostel on *Paracelsusstraße*. Michael gratefully flopped into a bed for the night. Now they were back on the road: Michael once again behind Heinz, who was driving the coach from the previous day.

"I'm not sure I understand," said Michael. "How do we still have this coach?"

"It's a short term loan," said Heinz airily. "We just need it until we get to Geneva, yeah? Anyway, it means that I can drive while Aisling works on the song."

Michael moved seats, joining Aisling. She pored over a notepad. "So how's it going with the song?"

Aisling flipped through the notepad. "I've left the Danube well alone for now. Listen, it's a tough call, coming up with something to unite the whole of Europe, but there's one thing I think all Europeans have in common at the moment."

"What's that?"

"A fear Donald Trump might win the American election. Is there any way we can use that, do you think?"

Michael thought hard for a few minutes. "On the face of it, it's a negative sentiment, and I'm not sure that would sit right. On the other hand, you have a very good point about it being a common thread across Europe."

Encouraged, Aisling turned to another page and cleared her throat.

"Run with me, don't be late,
"You don't need a wall to make America great."

"That's excellent, although you just need to change 'running' to 'flying'. That should be fine then."

"Fine?" said Aisling. "And how will it be fine?"

"It's there in the Eurovision statistics," said Michael. "Walking and running is something that losing songs have in them. Nine in recent years, would you believe? Flying's different though. Six recent winners have used flying in their songs. Is there any more?"

Aisling nodded and continued.

"Stand with me, come and see,
"The lesser of two evils is Hillary."

Michael nodded in appreciation. "It's catchy. Extremely catchy and very topical. But I think that might be its downfall. In a week's time, it'll be out of date. The election will be over."

"I'll tweak it, obviously," said Aisling, somewhat defensively. "Ooh, Sweet Jesus, will you look at the drop there!"

She was staring out of the window, to where the mountainside fell away into the depths of the valley below, shrouded in mist. Michael made his way back up the bus and sat behind Heinz again.

"Challenging roads," he remarked. "I bet you never faced things like this when you took your PSV test."

"What's a PSV test?" asked Heinz.

"Maybe it's called something different in Finland. It's the special qualification to let you drive a big thing like this."

"There's a qualification?" said Heinz. "Who knew."

Michael laughed. "Oh, you are funny, Heinz. I know you're joking."

"To be honest, my friend, I just figured it all out yesterday when I stepped behind the wheel."

"But there's no way the tour company would lend you a coach if you weren't even qualified to drive it..."

Michael sat back in his seat and considered his words as the coach swerved around a hairpin bend. "Heinz," he whispered hoarsely. "You don't have permission from the coach company do you?"

"Hey, it's fine," Heinz said, waving a hand. "Those people on the tour had the time of their lives yesterday. The company will get their coach back when we're done. It's a victimless crime."

"It's only a victimless crime as long as we don't fall off the side of the mountain," croaked Michael, his fingers gripping the edge of the seat in terror.

Hours later, Michael was still rigid with fear, even though some part of his brain had registered the transition from terrifying mountain roads to major, blessedly flat thoroughfares. Todor waved a bag of tomatoes in his face.

"Come on Michael, you had tough couple of days, but we are arrived now! Here at the headquarters of the European Broadcasting place, home of Eurovision!"

Michael walked stiffly off the bus. Even though he would not be troubled by a tumble off a mountain, being responsible for the deaths of a coachload of mortals would be an intolerable burden. Yet, by some miracle, they had made it to Geneva and now it was up to him to convince the heads of Eurovision to bring the competition forward.

The European Broadcasting Union's headquarters were a pair of drab, late twentieth century office blocks. A glass walkway connecting the two buildings was plastered with huge letters, proudly declaring this to be the home of Eurovision.

Like Moses at the shores of the Red Sea, like Noah atop Mount Ararat, Michael felt a swell of pride as he neared his goal. On legs quivering with excitement, he approached the receptionist and turned on the full wattage of his most charming smile. "Good day to you!"

"Good morning, sir," said the Swiss receptionist in smooth English.

"I need to speak with the head of the Eurovision Song Contest, please. It's a matter of urgency."

The receptionist gave him a blank look, fingers poised over a keypad. "What name is that?"

"Sorry?"

"The name of the person with whom you have an appointment?"

"I don't have an appointment, but I need to speak with the person who's in charge of the Eurovision Song Contest."

"You need an appointment," she said. "I can't let you in without one."

"Right," said Michael, still smiling. "Could I make an appointment?"

"Sir, I'm unable to make appointments for executive members. You will need to speak with one of the private secretaries."

"No problem," said Michael, his smile faltering a little. "Would you please put me through to one of the private secretaries?"

"Sir, I don't have a phone here that is cleared for members of the public to use."

"In that case, would you please give me the contact details for one of the private secretaries?"

"What name?"

"Well I don't have a name. Perhaps you could tell me one?"

"Sir, I'm afraid our information security policy does not permit me to give out personal information about our employees."

Michael took a deep breath and willed away the mounting frustration. "Right. But if I wanted to speak to someone about the Eurovision Song Contest...?"

"You can speak to me, sir."

"Do you have responsibility for the running of the contest?"

"No, sir." She smiled. "That would be the executive members, or one of the private secretaries."

"Yes. So, could I speak to one?"

"Which one?"

"Whoever is running the show."

"That would be down to the host nation broadcasters. In Kiev. That's in Ukraine."

"I *do* know who is hosting the next Eurovision Song Contest, madam," said Michael indignantly. "What kind of fool do you take me for?"

"What kind of fool would you like me to take you for?"

"If I wrote a letter and addressed it to the head of the Eurovision Song Contest, would it be opened?" he asked.

"Not until March, sir. Correspondence will not be looked at until three months before the contest, which isn't until June. Will that be all sir?" she said, clearly dismissing him.

Michael's legs quivered some more, not with excitement this time but anger. He clenched his phone furiously. What was it Mark Twain had said? When angry, count to four. When very angry, swear. Michael counted to four. He then counted some more because it clearly wasn't working.

"Why are you counting, sir?" said the reception, mildly alarmed. She looked at his face and the phone in his hands. "Sir?"

She reached for a phone. By her body language, Michael could tell it was going to be the kind of phone call that might result in another stay in police custody.

He left the building and trudged back to the coach, a broken man.

He climbed onto the coach and addressed the hopeful faces that were turned towards him. "Bit of a delay, everyone," he said with the best fake grin he could muster, "but it's no problem. We will use the time to get the song ready and hone our performance skills." He dropped into his seat so he wouldn't have to face them all, the lies surely obvious from his face. "Let's go, Heinz."

"Sure thing, Michael. Where to?"

Michael sighed and spoke quietly. "I'm not sure, Heinz. Truth is, I didn't even get to talk to anyone inside there."

"The Swiss can be such cocks," said Heinz.

"They wouldn't even listen. Blocked me at every turn."

"Cock blockers."

I feel as if I've let everyone down. I've brought you all this far, but I don't think we can get our song out to Europe in time. Now, I just don't know what to do."

Heinz let the engine idle for a moment. He turned it off and came round to sit with Michael. "Listen to me. You have a crazy dream, right? My speciality is crazy dreams. Let me help you make this thing happen. It will be all right, I promise. In the meantime, I know you want to get some of the stinky local cheese, so let's go and find ourselves a picnic!"

Everyone walked around *La Halle de Rive*, an up-market foodie destination in central Geneva. At first, they looked a little intimidated (apart from Todor who immediately found some tomatoes to pass judgement upon). Michael put his hands in the air to get their attention.

"We need picnic supplies for a day or two. Everyone grab what you'd like. I'm paying."

There was a sudden scramble. Baskets of shopping were brought forward in rapid succession. Michael sampled various wares, adding wheels of raclette, gruyere and a wonderfully pungent Vacherin Mont d'Or to his own basket. At least one of them should last until he got home and could share it with Andy. He sighed as he thought of Andy and rattled off a quick text.

Failed to achieve our goals at EBN headquarters. Stockpiling supplies now – prepare for some noxious goodies later! Heinz and I will come up with a new plan, God willing. We will prevail! ☺

Reno, Nevada

Clovenhoof had been to casinos before. It was heartening to know that the casinos in Reno were like the casinos back in England: full of people who thought they were card sharps or smooth-as-fuck James Bond types, all trying to live out their personal fantasies in a place that had as much class and charm as a Blackpool amusement arcade.

There were three things that Clovenhoof loved about casinos. One, he was the devil and it was pretty much a given that he would win any game of chance he chose to play. Two, as long as he kept playing, he could stay indoors. A stool at a blackjack table was hardly a bed but he had at least spent the night and the morning in the windowless, air-conditioned cocoon of the Ariana Casino Reno. And three, he was currently enjoying the delights of limitless prawn buffet. As long as he played, the wonderful Mitzy, who was working the Ariana's graveyard shift, would keep the stuff coming. When he phoned up the Guinness Book of Records regarding his constipation challenge, Clovenhoof thought he should also ask about the world record for continuous prawn consumption.

He picked up the prawn on his plate and invited it to look at his cards. "What do you reckon, Percival?"

The headless prawn gazed at his cards. A jack and an eight.

"I hear you," said Clovenhoof. "Only a fool would take another card with a hand like that."

"Jeremy," said the dealer. "What have we told you about talking to the shrimp?"

"Sorry, Randy." Clovenhoof popped the prawn in his mouth. "Hit me."

91

The dealer flipped him a card: a three. He caught the smile on Clovenhoof's face and sighed.

"Don't worry," said Clovenhoof. "You're going to get the biggest tip when I'm done. Mitzy! More prawn!"

The three men latched onto Clovenhoof the very moment he stepped out of the Ariana Casino. Maybe it was because Clovenhoof was an obvious out-of-towner. Maybe it was because he was whistling, laughing and skipping at the same time. Maybe it was because of the wads of cash that just didn't want to stay in his bulging pockets.

At the corner of the Ariana Casino building, one of them stuck something hard into the base of Clovenhoof's spine and said, "Into the alley."

"Jeez. Haven't you heard of Grindr? This is not how you meet guys these days."

A firm hand on his shoulder steered Clovenhoof round the building and down a side alley lined with loose and bagged garbage.

"I'm flattered of course," said Clovenhoof. "But I've got places to be, elections to stop."

One of the men shoved him brutally against a wall between two dumpsters. He turned Clovenhoof round, slamming him back against the wall a second time. There were three in all: one tall, one short, one fat. It was almost as if they had held auditions for the roles. The tall one held the pistol.

"Give it to us," said the short one.

"In England, it's called cottaging," said Clovenhoof conversationally, "and traditionally it takes place in public toilets. The smell is hardly romantic, but at least it's inside in the dry. An important consideration over there."

The fat one slammed a fist into Clovenhoof's gut, doubling him over.

"The cash, dickwad," repeated the short one.

Clovenhoof straightened up with difficulty. "Don't do that again," he said to the fat one, "or you'll regret it."

There was something infuriatingly delicious about the human psyche, thought Clovenhoof. Among large swathes of society, if you told a person, "Don't you dare do X" they would immediately do X out of spite, oblivious to the Y and Z that might follow.

In this instance, X was a punch to Clovenhoof's gut. The Y was Clovenhoof vomiting up fifteen hours' worth of free casino prawns and beer all over the short, tall and fat muggers. The short one was unfortunately positioned with his mouth open. The Z was Clovenhoof running away, the short mugger screaming like he'd stuck his face in a blender, and the remaining two torn between giving chase and jiggling about in disgust at what Clovenhoof had done to their nice clean mugging clothes.

Lake Geneva, Switzerland

Heinz found a camp site near to Lake Geneva with pre-erected tents. The group settled in, lit the fire pits and ate some of the fragrant offerings from *La Halle de Rive*. Michael felt particularly pleased with the fondue he created from his gruyere: melting it on the fire pit. Todor was very happy to dunk tomatoes into the hot cheese, announcing it was delicious. Soon everyone was dipping in a selection of their own purchases, although Michael was perplexed at Ibolya's dipping chocolate in cheese. Stefan had bundles of strong, cured sausages which provided an intriguing counterpoint to the molten gruyere. A distinct and pungent haze shimmered in the air; Michael considered it fortunate their group was alone in the campsite.

"You guys! You should get out your instruments and do some jamming, yeah?" said Heinz, standing. "I need to pop out for a short while."

Heinz drove away in the coach as Stefan tuned his guitar. Ibolya sang some scales and Todor responded with snippets culled from *The Aristocats' Scales and Arpeggios*, much to her annoyance.

"You two must learn to sing together!" said Aisling. "Let's find a duet that you both know, and you can warm up by singing it."

"How about *A Whole New World*?" suggested Todor.

"Never heard of it," said Ibolya scornfully. "Something like *O sink hernieder, Nacht der Liebe* from *Tristan und Isolde* might be more fitting, perhaps?"

"I don't know any of that fancy stuff. Do you know any pop duets?"

Ibolya sighed. "Something like *Dead Ringer for Love* by Cher and Meatloaf perhaps?"

"Yes!" said Todor.

Stefan strummed some opening chords.

"Very well," said Ibolya, "but I want to see your heart and soul in the performance, yes?"

"You got it, baby!"

Michael sat back and admired his super group coming together. He was familiar with the song they were singing, but he didn't remember so much tomato-based flirting in the video. On the whole, though, it seemed as though there was real chemistry here.

Aisling clearly thought so too, directing the band on their imaginary stage in Heinz's absence.

"Stefan, I want to see much more moody pouting from you! There's a time for looking like an eager puppy, but it's not now. Todor! A little *less* twerking, perhaps. It's a bit too 2013 don't you think? Ibolya? I can see you like to have something to do with your hands, but we need to keep this family friendly. Maybe we'll get you a tambourine, so."

"You know, this might just work," said Michael. "Europe united by song, and Great Britain drawn back into the European family."

Stefan grunted in amusement. "You know, I never really imagine the United Kingdom as part of Europe."

"For shame," said Ibolya. "It is a much valued and signed up member of the Union."

"I know that," said the lawyer, as he gently plucked lullaby riffs on his guitar. "I mean I don't see it as an essentially European place. It lacks a certain something ... a *je ne sais quoi*."

Michael saw the twitch in Aisling's eye. "Easy on the multilingualisms, Stefan," he said.

"So, what makes it un-European?" asked Ibolya.

"Is it because it's an island *off* the coast of Europe?" said Aisling.

"Partly."

"But you don't think Sardinia or Corsica are un-European?"

"Yes, but the United Kingdom is stuck way out there: on the edge of things."

"And what about Ireland?" said Aisling.

"Isn't Ireland part of the United Kingdom?" asked Todor, innocently.

Michael sat upright in case he needed to stop an Irish patriot attacking the Bulgarian but all Aisling did was fix him with a hard stare and say, "Men have been shot for saying less than that, Todor."

"But what about places like Iceland?" Ibolya asked Stefan. "Far to the north west. Is that European?"

"I don't know," said Stefan. "The British. It is like they are fifty-percent American and fifty-percent I do not know."

"American culture permeates all countries these days," said Ibolya. There was the sound of five people muttering in miserable agreement. "I don't think you can say the UK is any less European than anywhere else."

"But I know what he means," said Michael, "and I live there."

"You know," said Todor in the dark quiet, "when I am faced with an issue like this, I always ask myself one question: what does the tomato teach us?" He held aloft one of his prized toms. "We ask, is it a fruit or is it a vegetable? It has seeds like a fruit but you would be fool to put it in a fruit salad. It is sweet to the taste but we use it for sauces with our main dish. Is it fruit, is it vegetable? We argue over words but, in the end, the tomato remains a tomato."

The fire pits burned low.

Reno, Nevada

With his fresh gaming wins, Clovenhoof took a taxi to the Reno-Sparks Convention Centre that evening. Best as he could tell, the Trump supporters of Nevada were very much like those he had met in North Carolina. A little bit less redneck, a little bit more cowboy. Red *Make America Great Again* baseball caps were very much part of the uniform for the die-hard Trump fan. As he mingled, Clovenhoof wondered what the correct noun was for a Trump supporter. Back home, supporters of Margaret Thatcher had been Thatcherites. Jeremy Corbyn had his Corbynistas. What was a Trump advocate? Trumpist? Trumpette? Trumpoline?

Clovenhoof worked his way through the buzzed up Trumpettes to the front. He slipped past a man waving a *Hispanics for Trump* placard, and occupied a spot next to a bald guy in a thick coat.

Clovenhoof gave the man a nod of greeting, which the man warily returned, but Clovenhoof didn't engage him in conversation. He needed to keep a low profile until the right moment. He had to keep out of trouble until Trump took to the podium and gave Clovenhoof an opportunity to speak to him directly.

Clovenhoof's plans so far had failed. He couldn't rubbish the man's character or ruin his good name; Trump had aired all his dirty laundry in public already and the great American electorate didn't seem to care. Clovenhoof couldn't drive wavering voters away by revealing the extremist attitudes of the core Trumpists; the mad, racist, sexist, xenophobia Trumpettes weren't camera shy and the American public had seen them in all their backward-looking, blindly-simplistic glory.

Clovenhoof's new plan had to succeed and he had brought his two weapons with him. In one hand, he held his copy of Nostradamus' Apocalypse Bingo with fifteen of the dire prophecies crossed out. In the other, he held the abominable bar of Toblerone that had set them on this final desperate race to save the world.

Trump did not come on immediately. Just like any headliner, he had his warm up guys. Some be-suited local came on and, to much inexplicable cheering, wittered on about forty-six thousand something-or-others and declared "Election day is Elephant Day." Then, not much better, a bespectacled geezer took to the stage, ranting about the FBI and how the judiciary should convict Hillary Clinton of that vague crime of hers involving e-mails (Clovenhoof wasn't sure if the e-mails she had supposedly hidden were lesbian love notes, assassination plans or instructions to her army of Hillary doubles; it really wasn't made clear by anyone at any point).

But finally, to the accompaniment of an electric guitar fanfare, the Republican candidate for the White House came out of the wings and greeted the crowd.

"We didn't bring any so-called stars along," he told the Nevada audience. "We didn't need 'em. You know, the reason Hillary has to do that is nobody comes for her. She can't fill a room. We can get stars. We don't need 'em."

"That's what I *said*," said Clovenhoof to no one in particular.

"Because we just wanna make America great again," said Trump, "and we know what to do, eh?"

The bald man next to Clovenhoof grumbled at that. Which was odd, because most of the audience were enraptured.

Trump spoke and the crowd responded. "Crooked" Hillary. Rigged televised debates. The failure of Obamacare. Murderous illegal immigrants. The wilder the allegations, the louder the cheering.

And Clovenhoof (not usually one for intellectual introspection) found himself remembering Joseph Goebbels, Hitler's Minister for Propaganda. They had met once, back in the days when Clovenhoof still had the old Lord of Hell gig and went by the name of Satan. In Earth reckoning it would have been something like seventy years ago, not long after Goebbels had attempted to escape the final destruction of the Nazi dream with a cyanide capsule and a bullet. But Goebbels had only succeeded in swapping one hell for another.

Satan had met him in the Sixth Circle of Hell, where the iron-bearded and steel-taloned demon Scabass was getting creative with a Jewish menorah and a tub of petroleum jelly.

"And who is this?" Satan had asked.

"Joseph Goebbels, my Lord," Scabass had replied. "Adolf's right hand man and a dab hand at stoking the fires of hatred."

"Oh, I like these types," Satan had said. "Have you introduced him to our Fires of Hatred yet?"

"Not yet, my Lord."

"I think our Fires of Hatred are better. They're much more literal."

The horrible pale creature had sobbed, muttering, "It's not real. It's not real. It's not real."

"Scabass," Satan had said.

"Yes, my Lord?"

"Is this the man who said, 'If you tell the same lie enough times, people will believe it; and the bigger the lie, the better'?"

"Yes, my Lord."

"Interesting."

And Satan had leaned in close, to put his face next to that of the squirming man.

"It's not real," Goebbels snivelled. "It's not real."

"You keep telling yourself that, Joe," Satan had said and walked on without a backward glance.

Trump was no Goebbels. He was either far cleverer or far more stupid. Where Goebbels stuck to one or two big lies, Trump's outrageous statements and accusations shifted and switched. It was almost impossible to point at one thing that he had actually, truly and definitely said. He mixed fact, hearsay, metaphor and hyperbole to such a fine degree it was impossible to seize on a quote that could be used against him. In truth, Clovenhoof was impressed.

But his opinion of the man didn't matter. Clovenhoof had a world to save.

He waved the Apocalypse Bingo sheet in the air. "Mr Trump! Mr Trump! You need to stop!"

People nearby looked at him but, close though he was, the noise in that hall was too much for Trump to hear him.

"Trump! You have to drop out of the election!"

"What are you sayin'?" said a man behind Clovenhoof and gave him a shove.

Trump did at least see the altercation in the crowd and peered down. "We have one of those guys from the Hillary Clinton campaign," he joked to the audience. "How much are you being paid? Fifteen hundred dollars?"

"No, you have to listen!" Clovenhoof shouted. "The world is going to end!"

"All right. Take him out," said Trump.

Security guys, all dressed like they were on their way to a Reservoir Dog fancy dress party, moved through the crowd towards Clovenhoof. The man behind him gave him another shove.

"When we win the election on Tuesday," Trump continued to the crowd. "You will finally have a government on your side. Fighting for your community and protecting your family."

The security guys – secret service, private security, Clovenhoof wasn't sure – closed in and went straight past him to the shoving man.

"Not me, him," said the man as he was led away.

Clovenhoof, chuffed by his good fortune, smiled to the bald guy to his left. The bald guy unzipped his thick coat. There was something stuffed under there, a folded sign or something similar.

"By the way, folks," said Trump, "while we're at it—" He paused and, hand shading his eyes against the spotlights, squinted at Clovenhoof who was capering and yelling.

"For the sake of the people, you have to quit!" yelled Clovenhoof. "Look! The fifteenth sign! They changed it!"

The bald guy in the thick coat, opened up his banner to hold it aloft but it was Clovenhoof who now had his attention.

Great—" said Trump, perhaps not sure what Clovenhoof was waving and pointing at him. Maybe they didn't have Toblerone in the States.

"Gun!" someone screamed.

"What?" said Clovenhoof. "No, it's a—"

"Gun!"

And suddenly the security guys were on the stage, holding up their arms to shield Trump, pushing him into a crouch to rush him from the stage.

"Wait! Don't go!" yelled Clovenhoof.

But then the crowd swelled in. Someone body-slammed the bald sign-holder. Clovenhoof turned. A fist connected with his face. Something booted and unfriendly connected with his knees. He stumbled. And then an American, never one of the lightest nationalities, leapt on top of him and powered him to the hard ground.

6th November 2016

Lake Geneva, Switzerland

Michael was woken by Heinz at dawn. He seemed very excited: saying that he'd found a great place for them to shoot a video. Heinz's idea was to create a video that was so amazing that it would go viral on the internet.

"Boom! All of Europe sees what you have done! Perfect, no?"

Michael had been impressed by the idea. He knew the power of the internet, and was happy with the technical challenge of optimising their exposure online. Considerably more difficult was mobilising the team in the early hours of the morning. Heinz was insistent that they should arrive early, and by some miracle they were all on the bus, heading for the location of the video shoot. Heinz had acquired a camera from somewhere, and Michael had spoken to him quite firmly: suggesting that filming their route was perhaps something the driver should not do. Instead, Stefan had been placed at the front to capture their journey.

They pulled off the main road at a tall fence. Heinz drove right up to it. He hopped down from the coach and dragged a section of it aside. After driving the coach through he dragged the section back into place. They drove on for a short distance before pulling up outside a nondescript grey building.

"This place is a little boring!" said Todor from the back seat. "No good for video here."

"Be patient!" said Heinz, leaning round to wink at them all. "You will see why this place is so perfect. Now we must all get off the coach and go inside the building. Make sure you take all of your things."

They trooped out with their backpacks and bags, and stood behind Heinz. He produced an electronic key pass from his jacket and used it to release the door lock.

"Hey, it worked!"

"You sound surprised," commented Michael.

"Come on in, folks. There should be nobody here early on a Sunday morning," said Heinz.

They walked through an empty reception area and corridor into a large room with many computer terminals. Michael realised it was organised into four distinct areas, each arranged in a circular fashion. From above it would resemble a clover leaf. There were displays above their heads, showing various charts and graphs. Michael looked at the enormous logo in the corner and gasped.

"Heinz, are we in CERN's control room?"

"We certainly are!" Heinz said. "We have the day to ourselves, yeah?"

Michael was about to query further, but he spun around to see why Aisling was making a strange gurgling noise. The grin on Aisling's face assured Michael she wasn't having some sort of seizure. He snapped his fingers in front of her eyes just to be sure. "What's the matter?"

"It's perfect, so." Aisling breathed. "The large hadron collider! The one thing all of Europe has that it can be proud of! Even America with its fancy Silicon Valley and Kennedy Space Centre hasn't got one of these!"

"Well actually—"Michael began.

"It's gorgeous. It's huge. It's— Exactly how huge is it?"

"Twenty seven kilometres," said Stefan automatically. "In two giant loops under Switzerland and France."

"The song must be about this!" said Aisling. "Quick! I need to get it down now!"

They scrambled to find Aisling paper and pens. For an office, it wasn't all that well stocked with stationery, Michael noted. Todor retrieved a folder from a high desk. It was a ring binder containing many pages of dense text and figures, printed single-sided. Todor handed a page out to everyone so they could jot down ideas to help Aisling. He also handed round a selection of herbal liqueurs that he'd picked up from their shopping trip the day before.

"To assist the creative process. It is made by monks!" he said. "Very healthy."

It was silent for a few minutes until Aisling made a small crowing noise. "Would you believe now that *super collider* rhymes with *health care provider*?"

Michael stared at her, confused. "How does that help? Anyway, it's the *large hadron collider* not the *super collider.*"

"Sure, I know that," said Aisling. "But I'm thinking of the song. *Super collider* sounds like a pop song. Like Abba's *Super Trouper,* yeah? Trust me, we call it that and we've got ourselves a winner."

"I follow your logic," conceded Michael. "However I feel compelled to point out that any song containing the lines *health care provider* sounds like a loser to me."

"Ah, maybe you're right," said Aisling, scribbling ever faster, covering the page.

"Does it have to rhyme?" asked Ibolya. Michael leaned over to look at her page. She'd written *supercollider* at the top and then followed it with *spider? cider?*

"Well now," said Aisling, looking at the ceiling to frame what she was about to say. "It's generally better if the bulk of the song is formed of rhyming couplets. A simple jaunty rhythm will generally follow on from there. What can work quite well though is if we have a bursting crescendo about two thirds through. You know the sort of thing. The act will be crouching down and jump up going *Ohhhhhh!* Now that'll be your moment for a witty standalone line, if you have one. Do you have one?"

"No, just asking," said Ibolya, vigorously crossing out her efforts. "Perhaps I will practise my yodelling. I assume the song will feature yodelling? It was, after all, the main feature of my hit single, *Bang Bang my Boom Boom.*"

"There will be no yodelling," said Aisling. "It's a novelty too far, I'm afraid."

"How can you dismiss yodelling as a novelty?" spat Ibolya, slamming down her paper. She stood up and flounced away from the group.

"Fine," said Aisling. "We'll open with a little low-key yodel. How would that be?"

"Don't patronise me!" snarled Ibolya, bringing her hand down hard on the console beside her. Everyone jumped as a mechanism whirred into life and a trapdoor slid open in the floor.

"Er, is there a label on that button you just pressed, Ibolya?" asked Michael. He had seen too many James Bond movies to know good news rarely followed an automated trap door.

"It says *emergency access LHC,*" said Stefan.

"Supercool!" yelled Heinz and scurried down a metal ladder.

Michael peered into the gloom. He decided he'd kick himself if he didn't take a look. Aisling was already descending; Stefan following close behind.

Michael looked at the others. Ibolya and Todor pulled a face at the prospect, but they joined him anyway.

Michael checked the control panel. Where Ibolya had hit the button there was another next to it that said *lights*. He pressed it, and a chorus of grateful exclamations came up from the hole. He stepped onto the ladder and followed Stefan down into a steel-lined shaft. At the bottom he was disappointed that the famous large hadron collider wasn't anywhere to be seen. Instead it was some sort of equipment room, with protective clothing lining the walls, and a small fleet of electric vehicles plugged into charging points. The others had wasted no time in unhooking three of these and were gleefully manoeuvring them around to face a tunnel leading off the room. Michael hopped in one with Aisling before she could pull away. They sped down the tunnel until it opened out into a much larger space.

"It *is* the large hadron collider!" said Michael, looking in awe at the famous curved tunnel. "Drive carefully everyone!" He was conscious the others were still swigging from bottles of Todor's dubious herbal spirit as they bowled along in the little buggies. There were complicated bits of tubing and wire all over the place, most of which did not look impact proof.

"Hey we should get some footage of us in here," shouted Heinz. "A little bit like the classic band shot where they drive over the sand dunes in beach buggies, yeah?"

They arranged the buggies in a neat procession. Michael climbed out of Aisling's and videoed them zooming playfully around the curve of the tunnel.

"I'm going right round," yelled Aisling. "I'll see you in a minute!" She disappeared around the bend.

"How long did you say this tunnel was?" asked Michael.

"Twenty seven kilometres," said Stefan.

"I don't know how long the battery lasts on these things, but I think she'll be gone for a while."

"So let's go back up top and work on the dance routine," said Heinz.

"How can we have a dance routine until the song is finished?" Michael asked. "Surely it will need to fit in with the song?"

"We can fine tune when Aisling's done," said Heinz, "but I think we can make a few basic assumptions about what the song's likely to have in it. What do you reckon, everyone?" he addressed the group. Stefan raised a hand.

"It will involve going round?" he ventured.

"No need to raise your hand, Stefan, we're not at school now. Anyway, well done, yes! Ibolya?"

"It will involve a bursting crescendo," she said with a roll of her eyes.

"Very likely!" said Heinz. "Come on everyone, let's go and make beautiful art with our bodies!"

Reno, Nevada

The secret service agents who had arrested Clovenhoof made him wait into the small hours in a small windowless room where the table and chairs were bolted to the floor. Clovenhoof spent the first few minutes pulling faces at the mirror that he knew from his movies would be one-way glass but there was little fun in making faces if you didn't know someone was looking.

Eventually, one of the Reservoir Dog-a-like agents, a big beefy fellow, came in and sat opposite Clovenhoof. He put Clovenhoof's Toblerone on the table, half of it now crushed to dust by the many feet which had also trodden Clovenhoof into the convention hall floor.

"I don't suppose you've also got the rolls of cash I had in my pocket, have you?" said Clovenhoof.

"What is this?" said the Dog.

"It used to be my favourite mountain-shaped chocolate bar."

"And why were you threatening Donald Trump with it?"

"Threatening? My good man, I was merely using it to illustrate the dire situation we are all currently in."

"Right." The Dog put a plastic pocket on the table containing the much crumpled Apocalypse Bingo sheet. *"The Trump of Doom will sound in victory, one week after All Hallows' Day."*

"Exactly," said Clovenhoof.

The Dog tapped the sheet. "This is stupid, sir."

"I wouldn't expect you to understand."

"What you did was very dangerous."

Clovenhoof automatically touched one of the bruises that had blossomed on his cheek and winced.

"You got off lightly compared to the other guy," said the Dog.

"What other guy?"

"The guy with the *Republicans Against Trump* sign next to you. He says he doesn't know you. He's lucky some of those *passionate* types didn't lynch him."

"Passionate. Yeah," said Clovenhoof, touching his bruise again and wincing once more.

"He's lucky a police officer or agent didn't shoot him."

"Tell me something," said Clovenhoof.

"What?" said the Dog.

"You're trained to protect the president or, you know, those who want to be president."

"That is correct."

"Would you leap in front of Trump and take a bullet if someone came at him with a gun."

"Yes, I would," said the Dog without any hesitation.

"You believe in him. You believe he's the answer to America's problems."

The secret service agent smiled. He actually seemed like an easy-going fellow. If he was a Reservoir Dog, he'd be a Reservoir St Bernards.

"I'm a Democrat, sir," he said.

"But..."

"I believe in democracy. Donald J Trump might or might not be the biggest asswipe who ever stood for office. I can neither confirm nor deny. But he's standing for office and I don't care what he's said or what anyone else has said, you don't change things with

105

violence, with a bullet. Not for the better, anyway." The Dog stood up. "This way, sir."

"Is this where you take me outside, shoot me and bury me in the desert?"

"There's no law against being a kook armed with a candy bar."

He led Clovenhoof out through the corridors of whatever grey and soulless municipal building they were in and to the front doors.

"Leave Reno, sir," said the Dog. "Please."

"The greatest trick the Devil ever pulled was convincing the world he didn't exist," said Clovenhoof. "And like that ... poof ... he was gone."

"We're letting you go," said the secret service agent. "You are not Keyser Soze."

"And like that – poof! – he was gone," Clovenhoof insisted dramatically. He banged his nose trying to get out of a locked emergency exit. Grinning sheepishly, he worked his way to the automatic sliding doors and out into the early morning gloom.

CERN, Switzerland

The dance class was a great idea, Michael decided. Heinz had rigged up the building's sound system to play pop tunes, and coached them all on some basic steps. It was immediately obvious Todor had a real problem remembering which was his left and which was his right. Ibolya used her lipstick to write an *L* and an *R* on his shoes to help him remember.

"You need to relax, Stefan!" called Heinz. "You look as if you're on a burning bridge above a vat of boiling oil! Loosen those shoulders! Own the stage, my man!"

Ibolya was adept at the routine, but Heinz complained at her habitually stomping her feet. "On your toes, Ibolya, on your toes!"

Michael enjoyed the step-two-three-thrust-and-kick routine. It was a pleasing type of discipline. He pulled out his phone and took a brief selfie of himself doing the thrusting motion. He'd send it to Andy later.

Heinz introduced a spin to the routine. He explained how stunning they would look, as they circled around the stage

106

mimicking the large hadron collider. He ignored the complaints about dizziness, saying they would soon get used to it.

"Todor, step to the left on my third count. One, two three. No, the other left! Oh God, the trapdoor!"

Todor's uncoordinated staggering took him to the open trapdoor and he stepped back into the void.

Michael gasped. How far down was the shaft? A hundred metres? He'd never survive the fall!

Todor's foot stepped on something – on nothing. There was an "Ow!" from below the hatch. Todor stumbled away, miraculously saved from death. Aisling emerged from the trapdoor, rubbing the top of her head.

"Bloody great eejit!" she grumbled. "Hey, did you know it's a really feckin' long way around that tunnel?"

Reno, Nevada

Clovenhoof knew he was running out of time. The election was in two days' time, he'd not been to the toilet in five, he had no cash or credit card, and Trump, despite all Clovenhoof's efforts, was neither discredited nor dissuaded. The polls still put Clinton miles ahead but Clovenhoof didn't trust either pollsters or the voting public to do the right thing.

At Reno-Taho Airport, after Clovenhoof confirmed that he couldn't get a flight for the four dollars and sixty five cents he had in his pocket, Clovenhoof made a phone call.

"Mason, I'm coming back to Florida."

"That's great, bro," yawned the Miami taxi driver. "How's Reno?"

"Hot. Deserty. I ate a lot of prawns, threw up and got my ass kicked by some Republicans."

"Sounds like Reno," Mason agreed. "When can we expect you?"

"I don't know," said Clovenhoof. "How soon can you get here?"

Mason laughed even though he knew Clovenhoof wasn't joking. "Good one, bro. What you need to do is get a flight."

"I can't."

"Then you'll have to do it cross-country. Car, coach. Beg, borrow, steal. I'm sure you'll manage it. We'll have boat drinks when you get here." Mason hung up.

CERN, Switzerland

As Michael closed the trapdoor, Ibolya comforted Todor, who was muttering darkly about the dangers of trying to tame his wild spirit.

"I know my love," she cooed, handing him a tomato. "Your unruly, passionate nature is a blessing and also a curse."

"I had a thought about the song while I was going the long way round," announced Aisling. They all looked at her expectantly. "Right, so. Now I wouldn't normally advocate this sort of thing, but time is tight, so maybe we need a shortcut. Who here remembers a song from the early eighties called *Torpedoes*? It was by a band called *Havana Let's Go*, if that helps?"

They all gazed back at her with an assortment of blank faces and shrugs.

"You don't remember it!" crowed Aisling. "Well let me tell you, it was a lovely little pop song. Perfectly crafted. The reason it got nowhere was Margaret Thatcher made the BBC stop playing it during the Falklands war. Well that's the rumour anyway. The point is, nobody remembers it. So I was thinking we take the song and adapt it for our purposes. I'm thinking we call it *Neutrinos*. Cool, huh? It will go like this:

"Neutrinos! Neutrinos!

"How I long to see you."

Michael waved his hands. She stopped, mid-flow. "Wait, wait, wait. Don't the rules of Eurovision say that the song must be original?"

"Sure, now," said Aisling "And the song *will* be original. Maybe somewhat derivative of *Torpedoes*, but nobody will know."

"*I'll* know," said Michael tapping his chest. "I couldn't possibly support an idea like that. We can't unite Europe based on a lie!"

"But it's fine to unite Europe by stealing a coach, blackmailing a receptionist with pornography and mucking about with one of the

108

world's most expensive scientific projects?" Aisling pulled a face. She huffed. "Grand. Well I need some sleep if I'm to come up with an amazing new song. I'm turning in for the night." She dragged a sleeping bag and bottle of Todor's dubious liqueur into a corner and curled up with her back to the rest of them.

"I believe that story about Margaret Thatcher," said Ibolya, taking a large layer cake from a carrier bag and sharing it out. "I'm afraid your country has always been a little bit crazy. Why else would they want to leave Europe? See this cake? It is of the sort that you can buy across many countries in Europe. Obviously the Hungarian *Dobostorta* is superior in every way, but Austria, Switzerland, Italy all have something similar. It is a delicate thing, made with skill and care. I went once to London, and asked in a bakery what cakes they had for sale. The thing they sold me was a stale bun with icing and a cherry on the top. Appalling!"

"There is good food to be found in England," said Michael defensively, "Although I know our reputation is not built upon it. It's the first time I've heard cake mentioned as a reason for staying or leaving Europe, though."

"The cake merely illustrates a wider malaise," said Ibolya haughtily. "An island nation that refuses to engage with its neighbours. Human rights? No thank you! Cheaper labour for the jobs you don't like? No thank you! It certainly looks like madness from my point of view."

"But Ibolya, you make it sound as if the rest of Europe gets along so well!" said Heinz. "It is very easy to observe that this is simply not the case. There are so many national stereotypes, and the petty grievances that go along with them. How will the people of Europe ever get along properly as long as we all believe that Germans are control freaks, Italians are crazy drivers and the French are a nation of sex maniacs?"

"And yet," said Todor, exchanging a look with Ibolya as she fed him a large scoop of cake. "And yet is possible to overcome this. We have so many things in common. This cake is good enough to overcome boundaries."

"Although it is not as good as Hungarian *Dobostorta*," corrected Ibolya.

"We know power of song can do the same," smiled Todor. "We have everything we need in this room to make Europe great again."

Stefan, who had been going through the carrier bags, scooted over as though he had something important to say. Michael was interested to know what his take on Brexit might be.

"I've looked everywhere for the last two bundles of those sausages, but I just can't find them," he said.

Reno, Nevada

Begging for a car failed. Borrowing a car was apparently not a thing. So, on Mason's advice, Clovenhoof stole one. Since he was in America, Clovenhoof thought he ought to drive like an American so he stole a big car that looked like it would go really fast and get really shitty gas mileage.

It ran out of fuel in Death Valley. There was no one else in sight in any direction so Clovenhoof lay down on the tarmac (which was scorching hot already, even though it was not yet nine in the morning) and played at being dead for a while. Something pecked at him occasionally but he ignored it. He only got up again when a truck pulled up in front of him and an elderly trucker called Truman asked him if he was dead or stupid.

Happy to confirm he was stupid, Clovenhoof jumped up and rode with Truman to Las Vegas, where Clovenhoof wisely stole a car with a full tank and good fuel economy. By nightfall, he had got as far as Flagstaff, Arizona. The most cursory glance at a map showed he had made barely any impact on the three thousand or so miles he needed to cover. He was nearer to Guatemala than he was to Florida.

"This is going to be an all-nighter," he told himself. He pulled in at a 7-Eleven, stocked up on Minotaur energy drinks and nicotine gum and hit the road to a classic rock soundtrack, courtesy of *93 Nine The Mountain* radio, cranked up to eleven.

7th November 2016

Somewhere in the southern United States

Clovenhoof screamed across America, literally. Around two in the morning, his bone-tired body had reached caffeine and nicotine saturation and the hallucinations kicked in. His eyes were so worn the world was reduced to blocks of colour which flew at him like some trippy hyperspace movie sequence. He shouted at imaginary road-users, failed to spot actual road-users, alternately freezing and sweltering as he switched back and forth between heating and air conditioning to keep himself awake.

Somewhere in Louisiana, Clovenhoof became convinced he was travelling faster than the speed of light. He was certain he had bypassed Mississippi completely. Pressed on the matter, he might have conjectured he had hit a bump in the road really hard, leapt clear over the Gulf of Mexico, and landed in West Florida. Clovenhoof's eyes, ears and brain had ceased to be reliable witnesses over a thousand miles back.

At some point he found himself having a telephone conversation with Mason the taxi driver. Clovenhoof couldn't remember who had called who or whether the phone call had ever truly happened.

"I've failed," said Clovenhoof.

"Failed, bro?" said Mason.

"I couldn't even get to speak to him. He wouldn't listen. I'm going to have to kill him."

"Kill him?"

"Terminate with extreme prejudice, for the sake of the world. And *Topless Darts on Ice*."

"Are you all right, bro? You sound super-spaced out."

"I've been driving for thirty hours without any sleep."

"That's not good, bro."

"I drank a lot of Minotaur energy drink. It turned my tongue blue."

"That stuff's lethal."

Clovenhoof swerved to avoid a big red blob that honked its horn at him. "It turned my piss blue too, Mason. My piss!"

There was a pause. "I thought you said you'd been driving non-stop, bro. Where did you—?"

"Piss? In an empty bottle. Now I don't know which bottles are which. They're all blue!" Clovenhoof grabbed a random bottle off the passenger seat and tried to gauge by its warmth if its contents were Minotaur or devil pee. He shrugged, took a swig and still couldn't be sure.

"You're gonna meet me in Sarasota at eleven. At the fairground. Trump'll be there."

"Sarasota. That hundreds of miles away from Miami."

"And you've got—" Clovenhoof squinted at the clock on the dashboard. It was just a blur. He put his face right up to the display until the luminous green nearly blinded him but it was still no good. "You have hours," he told Mason.

"I'm not coming," said Mason. "Pull over someplace and get some sleep."

"I need to kill Donald Trump."

"The police and secret service will shoot you before you get within a hundred feet of him."

"I've got a secret plan. I'm gonna sneak in. They won't even see me."

"Get some sleep, bro," said Mason. "Let's talk about this tomorrow."

"You don't believe in me, Mason," sniffed Clovenhoof. "We were supposed to be a team. Love, honour and obey. Did those vows mean nothing to you?"

Before Mason could reply, Clovenhoof killed the call and dialled another number.

"Wagwan," said a voice.

"Francis, it's me," said Clovenhoof.

"Who?"

"Jeremy Clovenhoof. I mean Professor Baboon. We shared a dooby at the poolside. You sold me some brownies."

"Dude!" said Francis in greeting. "How's it hanging?"

"I'm not sure anymore," he said. "Are you still in Miami?"

"No, dude. I'm back home."

"Sarasota?"

"Sarasota."

"Excellent. Remember you said that if I ever needed an elephant."

"Um. I might have done," said Francis. "I say a lot of stuff when I'm high, dude."

"I need an elephant."

CERN, Switzerland

Michael pressed the intercom button. "Yes?" he said.

"This is the police," said a voice over the speaker.

"Yes, I got that bit the first time," said Michael. "How can I help you?"

"We wish to speak to the leader of the group occupying the control room."

"Leader? Todor's doing lead vocals, whereas I suppose I'm more sort of management."

"Am I speaking to the leader now?"

Michael hmmed. "I'm not sure I'm happy with such a hierarchical definition. We're kind of going for a loose team or cell structure. But you can speak to me." He instinctively felt the conversation had got off to a poor and woolly start. Then again, it wasn't every day one was woken up after a night camping inside the large hadron collider by the voice of law enforcement demanding entry.

"And what is your name?" said the police officer.

"My name? "said Michael warily. "Surely that's not important. Is there a problem?"

"Sir, are you Michael Michaels?"

"Ye-es, Michael Michaels, that's me."

"And you're part of a cell of the, let me see, *All the Countries of the World*? That is the name you gave when you first contacted the European Broadcasting Network's representatives in London."

"What? No. I was speaking to Trish from *Song for Europe*. I said our band is like all the countries of the world."

"But you're not directly affiliated with them. I understand."

"Affiliated with whom? Is that a thing? What kind of an outfit do you think we are?"

"We understand from our Austrian counterparts that you were arrested two days ago for propagating fascist ideologies, and now you have barricaded yourself inside the CERN control room, with some accomplices, having deployed explosives in the entrance hall."

Michael leaned away from the microphone and addressed the others. "What are they talking about?"

Stefan pointed to a screen that showed CCTV footage of the entrance hall. There was a suspicious bundle on the floor between the front entrance and the control room. "My missing sausages," he said mournfully.

Michael peered at the screen. He had no expertise in the field of explosives, but they certainly looked dangerous.

"Oh for goodness sake!" he said. "Let's just set everything straight, shall we? Heinz, who was it gave us permission to come and film in here at the weekend?"

Heinz made a see-saw motion with his hand. "It wasn't *exactly* like that," he said. "It was more like a man sold me a pass and some bolt cutters in a bar, and told me where the fence was not covered by the cameras."

"Oh." Michael drummed his fingers on the edge of the console, finally realising how this might look from outside.

Heinz joined him. "You know, Michael, this isn't all bad. In terms of getting noticed, it's pretty good, actually."

Michael looked at the rest of the group. Ibolya and Todor were wedging chairs under the door handles, Aisling could be heard muttering excitedly about what might rhyme with *siege*. Only Stefan looked a little anxious.

"As your attorney," he said, "I must point out this could be very bad. Although, we might gain some legal wiggle room from the fact that we are in a cross-border situation." He stepped to one side. "France." He stepped to the other. "Switzerland."

Michael pondered. "We can use the opportunity to get our message out there," he said eventually. He turned back to the microphone, pressing the button. "Hello again. I want to tell you that we intend no harm to anyone with this small endeavour of ours, but we do have something we want to bring to your attention. Please listen to this message. It is our dream and our mission to see the unification of Europe, and we're starting that process today. Not far from here, not so long ago, some people had a dream of a Europe brought together under a single banner. We plan to rally together like them and create one people. Our belief in Europe is unshakeable and our will is overwhelming."

There was a long pause from the speakers, and Michael wondered if the link had been severed.

"We understand," said the police officer. "And do you have any demands that you wish to share with us now?"

Heinz indicated that Michael should let him take over the microphone.

"Yes. Our creative director will share that with you," said Michael, moving aside so that Heinz could speak.

"Hello negotiators! It's a pleasure to speak with you! I'm going to need quite a few things from you, so please have pencil and paper ready, yeah? Let's start with the dry ice machine. Got that? Also, we need TVs and cameras for the live broadcast. Actually, can you tap into CERN's CCTV and record it for broadcast? You can? Excellent. Hang on, my friend is flapping his arms at me." Heinz stared at Todor's mime. "Oh! Yes. Some doves." He winked at Todor. "We need a flock of at least twenty."

The day proceeded with more dance practices, even though they still had no song to dance to. Michael was gratified to see that the moves were starting to resemble dancing rather than the crew of a gale-tossed trawler trying to stay upright.

During lunch, Stefan managed to bring up a local news channel on one of the overhead displays. The newsreader was part way through reading a story, with an image behind her that showed them all in CERN's control room. The image was captioned with *CERN SIEGE - LIVE*.

"Oh look, it's us!" said Ibolya, regarding her image critically and tapping her nascent double chin as though it had let her down in the broadcast.

"The leader of the terrorist cell has been identified as Michael Michaels," said the newsreader, "a neo-Nazi travelling under a UK passport who was detained this week in Austria for alleged hate crimes."

"And rightly released," said Stefan.

"In his brief statement on taking over the CERN control room, Michael pledged to reunite Europe under a single banner."

"See?" said Heinz. "We're getting noticed."

"These chilling echoes of Hitler's fascist rhetoric," continued the newsreader, "are all the more alarming given that, as we see in this footage here, Michaels attempted to detonate a suicide bomb device at the European Broadcasting Network on Saturday."

"I did what?" spat Michael.

"Witnesses say Michaels, visibly agitated, demanded to see network executives and, when refused, gave a countdown and attempted to activate a device with his phone. It seems increasingly clear that the group will not relinquish the control room peacefully. We will bring you further developments as we get them."

"Well they've leapt to some wild conclusions there!" said Michael, annoyed. "Why on earth do they think I'm a neo-Nazi?"

"Michael, none of this will matter once we get the song and the video sorted," soothed Heinz. "Mind you, they're taking their sweet time bringing the stuff we asked for." He moved over to the microphone. "How much longer before the supplies arrive?" he barked.

"We will update you shortly," said the voice. "It's all being sourced for you."

Michael took himself away down a corridor to think. He couldn't help but feel things were a little bit out of hand. Perhaps Clovenhoof was having a little more success with his own mission. Unlikely, he thought. Clovenhoof was a walking disaster. In fact, thought Michael, already dialling Clovenhoof's mobile, it would do him good to put things in perspective and find out how appallingly Clovenhoof was doing.

Clovenhoof answered with a yell. "Mickey boy! Bad timing! Right in the middle of something here!"

There was a wild and piercing horn blast.

"What is that?" said Michael. "A trumpet?"

"No," yelled Clovenhoof. "That's Delores. A dynamite gal and our secret weapon. Francis assures me she'll get us past the secret service guys. Delores! Delores! This way! Look! Donuts!"

"Secret weapon for what?"

"What?" said Clovenhoof, clearly distracted.

"I said what secret weapon?"

"Delores!" shouted Clovenhoof, although whether that was directed at Michael or not, the archangel couldn't tell. "Francis! Get her over here! Bring that jumbo down so I get on top!"

"I'm trying, dude," came a distant male voice. "But she doesn't want to—"

The call died. Michael stared at the phone. Well, it certainly sounded like Clovenhoof was make a disastrously bad fist of things.

"Michael, can we have a word?" said Todor. He was with Ibolya. The pair of them stood hand in hand. They spoke quietly, clearly not wanting to be overheard by the others.

"Yes, what is it?" said Michael.

"Do you believe that Aisling will really create a song?" asked Ibolya, her face anxious. "You know we believe in your vision, but the stakes are higher now."

"Yes, I realise that," said Michael testily.

"I have a little song which I wrote myself," said Ibolya with a modest blush. "Todor thinks it's got a lot of potential, and it features yodelling, something I know I can deliver in a very powerful way."

Michael reached for a suitable response but found he was unable to simultaneously express reassurance all would be well, general encouragement for the creative pursuit of songwriting, and an absolute horror of yodelling. He settled for: "Oh."

Ibolya launched into her song. It was a powerhouse of incomprehensible ululations. Michael had a vague notion that yodelling had evolved as a method of counting sheep or some such; was he hearing a list of Hungarian sheep names? It somewhat resembled a recording he had once heard of a blue whale singing. He fretted that Ibolya's titanic rendition would frustrate the blue whales of the world, who would find themselves unable to navigate to landlocked Switzerland.

Todor was rapt throughout the performance, his eyes never leaving Ibolya's face. His expression was adoring and Michael wondered if he'd pushed something inside his ears. He didn't even flinch as Ibolya's voice reached a new high. Something in the control room smashed, but Michael didn't care, he just wanted the noise to stop. Eventually it did.

"Ibolya, that was really something," he stammered. His own voice sounded distant, his ears ringing with the aftermath of the trauma. "It could be a powerful standby, if Aisling is stuck."

He got up from the chair and tried to walk away, but his balance was affected. Halfway across the floor he met Aisling coming to meet him, similarly stricken. She clutched Michael's shoulder and ushered him across the room, casting terrified glances back over her shoulder.

"Promise me one thing, Michael. I know I've probably been a pain in the arse – what with not having a song and all – but please, promise me now that you won't let her sing that again?" She pleaded with her eyes. "I mean, maybe if they send in the Navy SEALS or something and it's a matter of life or death we could get her to— Or maybe we just take our chances with the Navy SEALS?"

Michael nodded weakly. "We need a song, Aisling. We really need a song."

"Yes! Give me a minute, so. Just a minute. I swear nothing focuses the mind like pain. I think I have something. I really do."

As Aisling scribbled on a pad, Stefan murmured, "They won't send the Navy SEALS in after us."

"It won't come to that, will it?" said Michael.

"No. The Swiss will send in the ARD10 commandos. Switzerland is landlocked. No navy, no SEALS. But ARD10, they're fierce mofos, Michael."

Not long after, Aisling put down the pen and nodded reverently. She nodded to Michael. "It's done."

"What? Already?" Could it be that simple? If Michael had known Aisling just needed to be traumatised, he'd have made her sit up front while Heinz drove through the mountains. "Can we hear it?"

Aisling nodded. "It's a song of two parts. There is the part like a thundering freight train. Todor will sing that. I saw how he sang and moved to the Meatloaf song. It calls for the same degree of subtlety. Anyway, Todor's part goes like this:

"Super collider, super collider
"Wondering if you know what will we find inside ya?
"Super collider, super collider
"Spinning round in circles, gettin' wider and wider."

119

Heinz appeared at once, jogging with high knees, fists pumping at his sides. "It has such energy! I love it!"

Aisling beamed. "Now we have the soaring operatic part, for Ibolya:

"Particle beams,

"It's like a river of dreams,

"We all hope and dream,

"Joining hands downstream

"Towards a love supreme!

"No yodelling, now," she added firmly "But Ibolya will bring power and drama to the delivery as we know she can."

Ibolya ran over and hugged Aisling. "Please let me sing it now! Todor, come here, we must try it immediately!"

They stood side by side and held Aisling's notebook between them. Todor winked at Ibolya, and Aisling counted them in.

As they started to sing, Michael found himself swept along by the energetic rhythm and the joy of the exchanges between Todor and Ibolya. They cycled through their two sections twice, and each time the pace changed it was like relay runners handing over the baton. No, it was more than that: it was like a pair of exotic birds on a wildlife programme. They circled and postured, in a loud and mesmerising courtship display.

"Beautiful," whispered Heinz as the song finished. "It will work so well with the routine and the costumes."

"There is one thing that's bothering me," said Michael. "You know the line about *River of dreams?*" It's immediately followed by *We all hope and dream.*"

"It is," said Aisling. "What of it?"

"Well it's not right is it?" said Michael. "How can you have a word rhyming with itself? It's like … cheating."

The entire group looked as if he'd suggested the ceiling of the Sistine Chapel might be better with a few glow in the dark stars applied to it.

"Michael, that's not the primary concern," said Aisling. "The heart and soul of the song is what matters. Nobody cares whether it will go down in history as a piece of poetry. Let it go."

Michael tried to put it from his mind, but he found himself considering other words that rhymed with *dream*, just to see whether there was an alternative. A river might reasonably be expected to have *bream* in it, but he couldn't imagine a fish themed diversion would go down well, so he kept that quiet.

A voice came over the intercom speaker. "We have the goods that you requested."

"Hey, our stuff has arrived!" shouted Heinz. "Come on, let's take a look."

They formed a human chain to bring boxes in from the foyer, and Heinz supervised the ones that they should open first. Michael watched Heinz extract lighting rigs and a dry ice machine. A series of large boxes yielded twelve flat screen televisions.

"How are you going to watch twelve televisions?" Michael asked.

Heinz tapped the side of his nose. "Michael, just you wait and see! Few extra bits of equipment to fix up these bad boys and then I will demonstrate."

Heinz spent a couple of hours fiddling with the electronics and finally announced he was ready to test his creation.

"So the first thing to do is for us all to get naked," he said.

Michael rolled his eyes. "Heinz, this has got to stop. I know you love the naked form but would you please focus? We need to get our Eurovision act sorted, maybe then you can talk to people about some naked street art."

"This is for the act!" said Heinz. "You wanted high tech wearables, yes?"

"That would have been nice," said Michael, "although I'm assuming it hasn't been possible?"

"On the contrary my friend," grinned Heinz. "Let me demonstrate."

Stefan had shed his clothes the moment Heinz mentioned getting naked. As a lawyer, he had demonstrated a certain Teutonic efficiency, but his attitude to personal nudity was nothing short of Scandinavian (and Michael couldn't help but notice Stefan's precise manscaping was confined to the neck up).

"Good man, Stefan," said Heinz. He lifted a large framework onto Stefan's shoulders. It had a flat screen television on the front and the back to protect Stefan's modesty, and he wore it like a sandwich board. At least he wore it briefly like a sandwich board: his knees buckled under the weight and he fell to the floor.

"Ah, slight problem there. Good job we have some smaller televisions. I'll rig you up with some thirty two inch ones. Todor! I think these might be better suited to you."

Todor and Ibolya had both disrobed and stood before Heinz, ready to have the bizarre television apparatus strapped onto them. Heinz helped Stefan to his feet and lifted the televisions off his shoulders. He put them on Todor and stood back to admire the effect. One television lay on top of Todor's vast belly, facing the ceiling.

"I might have to adjust the straps for you, I think."

He hung a set of televisions on Ibolya. He surveyed the effect and reached out to arrange her gargantuan chest. She slapped him.

"You want to arrange my body, you tell me what needs doing, and I will do it!" she said firmly.

Once Heinz was satisfied with his first three sets of wearable televisions he looked at Aisling.

"What?" said Aisling. "I'm not in the act."

"We're all in the act," said Heinz. "It's a question of solidarity. Clothes off, Aisling."

"You're feckin' kiddin' me," she grumbled, but stripped down to her knickers and bra nonetheless. "And these aren't coming off until I'm covered. Jesus, Father Fitzgibbon wasn't wrong when he told us rock 'n' roll would lead to nudity and debauchery."

"You too, Michael," said Heinz. "Get 'em off."

Finally, they all stood with televisions hanging fore and aft.

"Can I be the first to say that I think we all look like a bunch of eejits?" said Aisling. "I'm not seeing the point of this Heinz."

"Ah, the point will become clear momentarily," said Heinz. "You see each television has a wireless feed from this laptop, and we will play a cool video to complement our act. Watch this."

Heinz tapped a laptop key and started the video. He nodded to a monitor which he'd installed above their heads, showing the feed from a static camera. "This is how we are looking right now."

Michael saw the televisions had all lit up with images. Heinz had selected a video featuring a spectacular lightshow with fireworks and lasers. It made quite an impact. Heinz moved amongst them arranging people in height order and adjusting their straps so that the televisions appeared in a neatly staggered arrangement. Ibolya wriggled with discomfort, grabbing the edge of her television. Her display changed to show a newsreader.

"—details have emerged about the neo-Nazi terrorist group calling itself All the Countries of the World."

"Oh, what lies have they come up with now?" sighed Michael.

"Interpol has confirmed that their leader, Michael Michaels, was behind a cyber-attack on British intelligence at GCHQ and the French DGSI earlier this month."

"Well, hardly an attack," said Michael. "I left things as tidy as I found them. Tidier even."

"In a text communication with a British contact, Michaels referred to their failure to achieve their goals at the EBN headquarters, and spoke of their stockpiled resources including 'Some noxious goodies', a possible reference to chemical weapons. The text was signed off with an exhortation to God and a promise that they would prevail."

"Yes, well, they've clearly misconstrued that message," said Michael.

"And within the past hour," continued the newsreader, "intelligence agencies have intercepted a phone conversation between Michaels and an as-yet unidentified American contact in which they spoke of dynamite, secret weapons and a plan to bring a Jumbo down."

"Oh, for goodness sake!"

The newsreader put a finger to her ear. "We can go live to the security camera feed at CERN. It appears that, this evening, Michaels and his cell have been taking part in some sort of naked ritual. There is concern that they could be preparing for a Jonestown-style murder suicide."

The image flicked to live images of the barely dressed Euro-popsters, watching themselves on Ibolya's chest screen.

"Jesus, Mary and Joseph!" yelled Aisling, "They made it look like a feckin' orgy!"

Heinz grimaced and went to change the channel on Ibolya's television back. He got himself another slap before managing to find the correct button.

Sarasota, Florida

Mason Miller wasn't sure what ultimately compelled him to drive the two hundred-odd miles to Sarasota on the Gulf Coast. It wasn't like he felt a special attachment to that foreign guy, Clovenhoof. It certainly wasn't like he was a pledged signee to Clovenhoof's weird anti-Trump agenda (he would have to *understand* Clovenhoof's plans to be a supporter). Perhaps, he reflected, it was selfishness compelling him; particularly his fears of what would happen to his good self if Clovenhoof successfully gatecrashed Trump's rally, and the investigating forces discovered Mason had known about it in advance.

It would have been easier to phone the cops, or the Feds, and tell them that a former fare of his had told him he intended to kill Trump at the Sarasota rally. It would have been easier, but not in Mason's nature. He couldn't remember if Clovenhoof was a person of colour – he genuinely couldn't say what colour Clovenhoof's skin was – but the Florida police had a poor track record when it came to *not* shooting black men. Only a few months back, the Broward County guys had shot that man in his own back garden, one who'd been armed with nothing more offensive that a chicken wing and some fries. And Mason wasn't going to call the Feds: the FBI was part of Big Government, and they took too much interest in people's lives already.

So, Mason drove to Sarasota: two hundred miles without a fare. Not ideal for a Monday morning.

The Robarts Arena on Ringling Boulevard was part of the Sarasota Fairgrounds and fronted onto a massive parking lot. When the county fair was in, the place would be abuzz with rides and stalls and visitors from all across the Gulf Coast. Today, it was abuzz with Trump supporters, local law enforcement officers and purveyors of flags and fast food for the patriotic and hungry folks.

Mason got out of his taxi and stood on the inside edge of the door to give him an extra foot of height to scour the surrounding area for signs of Clovenhoof. He didn't have to look for long. There was something about a charging Asian elephant that really drew the eye.

It blundered across the parking lot from the general direction of the nearby zoo. Its head and trunk swung from side to side as it passed between the parked vehicles, sending new arrivals fleeing. On its side, someone had daubed the words *TRUMP – Make American Great Again* in white paint. On its back sat a familiar, wild-eyed individual.

"Delores!" yelled Clovenhoof. "Engage stealth mode!"

The elephant was, more by accident than design Mason assumed, charging straight for the front doors of the Robarts Arena. Mason could see clear as day what was going to happen. Either the cops and any armed Floridian in the area were going to take pot shots to stop the poor elephant's charge, or Clovenhoof would reach his target, burst through and cause untold deaths. For all that it was worth, Mason ran towards Clovenhoof, yelling for him to stop.

Clovenhoof couldn't hear him above the screams of those running away or the elephant's occasional trunky trumpetings. Up ahead, one of the cops by the arena building spotted the approaching animal and reached for his holster.

Mason screamed: both a warning and a yell of despair. It was all going to end very, very badly.

Thank God for the gift of donuts.

Clovenhoof woke with a brilliant headache and pains all along his side.

"Nnh!" he said in response to this intolerable situation and attempted to sit up.

"Easy, bro," said Mason from across the room.

Clovenhoof was laid out on a sofa. He was in a living room he did not recognise. A television in the corner had the sound turned down. The blinds were partially drawn and narrow stripes of bright sunlight speared into the room. Behind a breakfast bar partition was a kitchenette where Mason was cooking something hot and delicious on the stove.

"What happened?" said Clovenhoof.

"Lucky for you, Delores likes herself a donut, bro. Eggs?"

"Please," said Clovenhoof, creaking as he gradually sat up.

Mason scraped eggs onto two plates and brought them through to the living room. "They were gonna shoot you," he said. "I watched them. But then your elephant swerved and made a bee-line for a donut concession. She stopped. You didn't."

Clovenhoof tried the eggs. They were rubbery and watery at the same time, and utterly delicious. "I was trying to kill Trump."

"The only thing you killed was a donut seller's business. And that's a sin against God, bro. In all the confusion, I was able to get you out of there and back to *mi casa*."

Clovenhoof consulted his phone. There was a big crack across the screen where either he or possibly an elephant had landed on it. It was already afternoon on the last day before the election.

"Trump's left Florida," he said.

"Which is probably the best for both of you," said Mason.

"I've got to catch up with him somehow."

"You can't," said Mason bluntly.

"There's always a way."

Mason threw his fork down on his plate. "You know, bro. You know what you've never asked me?"

"What's that?"

"Never asked me who I'm going to vote for."

Clovenhoof gave Mason a look. Mason gave him a look back.

"Trump?" said Clovenhoof. "Really? But he's—"

"Yeah. He is," said Mason. "He is all of those things you're gonna say, bro, and if he lived round here I'd cross the street to avoid him."

"Then why?"

Mason beckoned with a finger. Clovenhoof followed him to the patio door where Mason pulled the blinds aside.

"See that, bro?"

Clovenhoof looked. "The swimming pool?"

"Damn right. I dug that. I built that. With my cash and my labour, I built that."

"It's a nice pool," said Clovenhoof. "I mean it's got no water in it but—"

"You know why it's got no water?"

"You can't swim?" Clovenhoof hazarded.

"Because the Department of Regulatory and Economic Resources says I can't until I've fitted a safety barrier. I built it, it's in my back yard which has a fence all round it, but I can't use it because the government says it's unsafe."

"And Donald Trump will ... let you use your pool?" said Clovenhoof, confused.

"It's not that," said Mason. "I look at Hillary Clinton and I think 'What has she ever built?' and then I look at Trump Tower in New York where Trump lives and I think 'he built that.'"

"I think he might have had some help."

"Point is, bro, the man gets things done. He's a builder, like me. He's a businessman, like me. He wants America to win."

"But he's a git."

"You think nice guys are winners? You think Steve Jobs was a nice guy. You think Winston Churchill was a nice guy. Donald Trump may rot in hell one day—"

"I'd imagine so," said Clovenhoof, speaking from a position of expertise.

"—but until that day, he's going to help America win, because America's best interests are his best interests. He doesn't want his own stock market portfolio to fall in value, bro. He's an honest crook but he's *our* honest crook."

Clovenhoof shook his head. "You'd elect him despite all you know about him?"

"Better the devil you know, bro," said Mason.

Clovenhoof thought about something Mason said and consulted his phone again. "I suppose you're right," he said. "Time for me to go home, huh?"

Mason gave him a genial shrug. "Do the right thing, bro."

"Can I have a lift to the train station?"

"Train station?" said Mason.

When the televisions were all stacked at the edges of the room and everyone had their clothes back on, Heinz pointed to a large unopened box in the corner. "Right, we need to check this out," he said. "This box contains our doves."

"Lovely!" said Todor. "Let's take a look at the beauties. I can hear them making gorgeous little clucking noises! "

They pulled the cardboard away and peered inside.

"I'm no ornithologist now," said Aisling, tilting her head critically. "But aren't those chickens?"

Stefan pulled a sheet of paper from the document wallet stuck on the crate's side. "It says 'We were unable to find two dozen white doves as requested, but you will be pleased to hear that under the terms of European Commission Regulation (EC) No. 2257/94, the enclosed domestic fowl are technically the same thing.'"

"What nonsense!" cried Todor. "They are chickens! What's more they are ugly chickens. They are not even white!"

"It seems they have addressed that," said Heinz, holding up a tin of white paint.

Michael had the feeling things were slipping out of control again. "Perhaps we can do without doves." The group faced him and he added hastily: "I mean, we need to get the act together and show it to Europe as soon as we can, or we run the risk of becoming quite disruptive."

"It will be a simple matter to paint these chickens if we share out the work," said Heinz. "Once that is done, we should get some sleep before we get things together for the final performance. Four chickens each, come on team, let's get painting!"

They air was filled with distressed clucking as they tried working out the best way to paint the brown chickens. Ibolya was the first to complete one. She fashioned an apron out of plastic packaging and clamped a chicken firmly to her bosom. She spread each wing and gave it a thorough coating. Todor poured some paint onto a paper plate and dipped his chickens into it, one side at a time. Aisling was slightly afraid to touch the chickens, choosing to dab a paintbrush at whichever part of the birds came near her. They ended up with a mixture of brown, white and variously piebald chickens. The only thing they had in common was looking very, very unhappy.

"Hey chickens!" said Todor. "You like yodelling? Maybe we cheer you up?"

"Chickens do not like yodelling," said Aisling emphatically. "Definite fact. It's well known, back in Ireland anyway, that chickens respond well to lullabies."

The rest of the evening was a bizarre blur of chicken-themed crooning, assisted by more of the mysterious herbal liqueur, which Michael began to suspect had psychotropic qualities. They started with *Rock a Bye Chicken on the Tree Top*, followed by a hearty chorus of *Shush Little Chicken* while Todor produced another bagful of tomatoes to munch on. There were several hampers of food which had been delivered along with the equipment, but Heinz voiced suspicions about whether it might have been tampered with, so they decided to leave it.

8th *November 2016*

The accidental terrorists awoke next morning full of enthusiasm for the task ahead, and hungry. Nobody aside from Todor wanted more tomatoes for breakfast. They examined the hampers again.

"It does look grand," said Aisling. "Fresh too."

"No one drink the Kool-Aid," said Heinz firmly. "We can't know if it's been messed with. Let's keep busy and put hunger out of our minds. We need to get a really great dress rehearsal done, and then I have arranged a live performance slot on all the television channels later on today. We can be ready for that, yeah?"

There was a chorus of agreement, driven partially by hunger. Michael had already heard Aisling suggesting one of the chickens might not be missed. It had been difficult enough painting the birds, Michael wasn't sure he was ready to endure their slaughter too.

Heinz stepped them through the routine while they were wearing their television wearables. The dance moves, limited as they were, were even more challenging when wearing hardware that weighed more than the baggage allowance for a budget airline.

Todor persisted in mixing up his left and his right, despite a fresh application of lipstick to his shoes. Quite a few of the televisions now sported cracks or had chunks missing after he had crashed into Ibolya and Michael, who had taken his place in the line-up at Heinz's insistence. Aisling gleefully seconded this decision, suggesting Michael should be the one to play the bucium, which had remained untouched in its case until now.

"It will be the perfect thing to open the song," said Aisling. "Like it's saying 'Pay attention Europe, here we come with our song'!"

"Why aren't you in the band?" Michael asked Heinz.

"Someone has to direct," said Heinz. "That will be me. Aisling is needed for production elements like working the dry ice machines and releasing the doves."

"Chickens."

"Yes, all right, chickens."

"I have noticed one thing about our chickens," said Michael. "They haven't shown any inclination to fly *at all*. I can't help thinking that when we release them they will just walk away. Weren't we looking for them to rise up into the air?"

Heinz winked at him. "Once again brother, I am ahead of you. I think we might almost be ready for full dress rehearsal, so let's do the dove thing for real. Help me unpack these drones and our chickens will indeed fly."

Once again, the air was filled with the sound of unhappy chickens as they wrapped them in webbing straps and clipped each bird to the underside of a drone. It proved tricky to keep the chickens upright; several did test circuits round the room listing at a strange angle, clucking mournfully. Eventually they had a full squadron of chickens attached to drones. Heinz created some nifty scripting on Michael's tablet so Aisling wouldn't have to try and work twenty four remote controls to get them all airborne at the correct moment. The same tablet controlled the images streaming onto the screens they were wearing. Heinz dubbed it Mission Control, and was fiercely protective of it.

"Dress rehearsal time!" called Heinz, lining them up in the correct position. "Get the bucium, Michael."

Michael fetched the unwieldly instrument from his case and eventually found a way to hold and support it while wearing the televisions.

"Everybody ready?" called Heinz. "Aisling. Mission Control is good to go?"

"Er, think so. Just trying to find the correct video file. And we're on low battery. Let me put it on charge."

Aisling took it to a control console, plugged the charger cable into the wall, turned it on and rested the tablet on the console.

"Okay, good to go."

Michael took his cue for a hefty blast of the bucium. He put his lips to the ancient wood and blew for all he was worth, but no sound came out. He took a deep breath and tried again until he felt the veins in his head standing out.

"This is possibly harder to play than it looks," he said.

"Um, what does that mean?" said Todor, pointing at an overhead display that had begun flashing red.

They looked up.

INITIATING START UP FOR THE LHC, PROGRAM 1

"Aisling?" said Heinz. "Did you turn something on over there?"

Aisling lifted up her tablet and looked at the rows of buttons and switches underneath. She gave a shrug. Michael joined her, in the hope that somewhere there would be a button labelled *Large Hadron Collider: On/Off.* He could see nothing that he could even begin to understand.

"We need to turn it off before someone notices," he said.

"Too late." Stefan pointed to the scrolling news banner on one of the TV screens.

LIVE: Terrorist group turn on large hadron collider. Analysts speculate that this is blackmail on a global scale. Do the group imagine they can create a black hole?

"Oh dear," said Michael. "Maybe we should talk to them."

"I think we might be beyond that," said Heinz. "Our video broadcast is in an hour. We need to barricade ourselves securely in place and get the song out. They will surely send in some sort of special forces if they think we're trying to blow up the world or something."

"They could just walk in the front door," Stefan pointed out. "The only reason that they haven't is because they think those sausages are explosives. They will just walk in and shoot us all."

"Which is why we must get the song out first, so that everyone understands what we're all about," said Michael. "I have an idea. Why don't we go down into the tunnel to do the song? We will be secure for a little longer down there."

Within moments they were lowering the equipment down through the trapdoor. It was exhausting work, but everything was in place in good time for their broadcast. As they stood next to the large hadron collider, it made a loud electronic humming, punctuated by occasional spitting noises that faded into a distant yowl.

"Is that going to interfere with the sound?" asked Michael.

"It adds atmosphere. It will be fine," said Heinz. "Everyone in position? The cameras are ready, and we're going to be feeding directly to the news channels that have signed up for this."

"Which ones?" asked Michael.

"All of them," replied Heinz with a broad smile. "Now, is everyone happy with the beats? I will give the signal for the start, and that's when you go with a nice loud blast on the bucium Michael. Aisling, you need to be ready to start up the video displays on the televisions, and to release the doves when I make this sign." He held up his hands with his thumbs linked and made a cooing sound as he made a flapping motion.

Aisling rolled her eyes and indicated that she was ready. Heinz flipped the switch on the dry ice machine, consulted his watch and counted them down.

This was it, thought Michael. A Brexit vote, followed by months of pained soul-searching on the madness of his adopted countrymen, followed by a few hours of frantic planning and a week of even more frantic travel around Europe to put together this Euro super-group: the Finnish lunatic, the Irish songsmith, the two singers, Bulgarian and Hungarian, the Austrian on guitar and he, Michael, representing the spirit of right-thinking British people with an alpine horn in his hand and TVs strapped to his naked body.

Yes, this was his moment. Here was their stand for European unity, their attempt to save the world and the open borders and free trade of a continent.

Michael had never felt prouder.

"Three, two, one. Michael!"

Michael made sure that he was looking directly into one of the security cameras as he blew into the bucium. He wanted the people of Europe to feel the sincerity of his gaze. The sound that came from the bucium was rich and clear, a siren call to everyone across Europe. Surely this would make everyone sit up and take notice? Todor started to sing, his voice easily drowning out the large hadron collider with its loud, raunchy delivery. They all stepped through the rhythm; Michael could feel the dance moves synchronising perfectly. Ibolya sang her operatic interlude and every soaring note was a new peak of perfection.

There was a noise with a different quality from along the tunnel. Michael tried not to be distracted. It was all so perfect, and they just needed to hold it together until the end, but then a dozen figures appeared: running around the curve of the tunnel from both ends. Michael kept his cool. Surely they would hold back until the song was finished? Couldn't they see what they were doing?

"Release the doves!" yelled Heinz. It wasn't time, but Michael understood the need to make their statement of peace while they were still able.

Aisling hit the controls and launched the chicken-carrying drones. The dozen figures, commandos clad in black and khaki, were briefly taken aback by the spectacle. They hadn't been trained to deal with drone-mounted chickens.

"Get the tablet!" shouted one.

A commando moved towards Aisling, but Ibolya stepped into his path. She was reaching the crescendo of her piece and she screamed the top note directly at him. He crumpled before her, staggered sideways, knocking into the large hadron collider. He fell against a lever which opened a small inspection hatch. Michael watched in horror as the flock of drone-propelled chickens flew directly towards the open hatch. The first of the chickens was pulled inside by unseen magnetic forces. The remains of the drone smashed against the side wall. Another chicken was drawn in. A few moments later, all of the chickens had disappeared.

Heinz shouted at Aisling. "The video feed, get the video feed up!"

Another of the commandos ran forward to take control of the tablet. He and Aisling wrestled for it. "Give it to me!" he barked. "*Gib es mir! Donne le moi!*"

His multilingual demands caused an instant rage to take over Aisling. She flew at the man, all fingers, nails and teeth. He screamed as she went for his eyes. Michael, agog, could only think the ex-lover who had once "Done her wrong" was very lucky to have avoided her in the intervening years.

Heinz dived for the tablet and stabbed at the screen just before it was snatched away from him by another commando. Michael smiled as their body screens lit up. A co-ordinated display of fireworks and lasers, illuminating this loyal and diverse group of people would make the statement that he'd pictured. They carried on with their dance steps, ignoring the special forces soldiers who now surrounded them, weapons raised. They just needed a minute more.

A strange sound came from the particle collider. It was a much louder version of the *phut–neeeow* it had been making previously. The sound approached them and Michael couldn't help turning his head to look, just as something small and deformed shot out of the open hatch. It struck the nearest special forces soldier on the back of his shoulder, propelling him with such force that his unconscious body was flung into their midst.

"Was that one of our chickens?" said Heinz. "Here comes another."

The remaining chickens came out of the large hadron collider like a poultry based Gatling gun. Todor's television screen smashed in a spectacular explosion of glass and plastic and sparks. The bag of tomatoes he had suspended between his screens for the purposes of snacking was instantly pulverised, showering down upon the fallen commando like so much blood. Todor danced to a different tune as he struggled out of the sparking and burning screen harness. There were flames elsewhere. The dry ice machine had taken a battering from where Aisling had used it to club a commando; now it was producing real, not fake smoke. Michael looked around. The group was in disarray, but the video feed was still playing on some of the screens. He froze when he realised the video was not the fireworks and lasers from before, but of Clovenhoof mincing about in a field and singing to a disinterested nanny goat.

"*I kissed a goat and it bit me*
"*The taste of her cud was delicious...*"

"No!" whined Michael. "No. Not that!"

As he watched, powerless to prevent the viewing public of Europe being subjected to the same spectacle, Clovenhoof snuggled up to the goat and nibbled her ear tenderly. Michael sank to his knees with a low moan.

"Make it stop! Make it stop!" he sobbed.

And then a chicken, flash-fried by a supersonic journey through subterranean Europe, shot out of the large hadron collider, smacked him squarely in the face and knocked him unconscious. Which, all in all, was a blessed relief.

New York, New York

The Amtrak Silver Meteor, at the end of its twenty six hour non-stop journey from Fort Lauderdale to New York, pulled in at Penn Station at seven o'clock on Tuesday evening, just as the polling stations were closing along the eastern seaboard. At eight o'clock, train officials found a man in an overhead compartment who claimed he had been forcibly stowed there by an individual who had stolen his ticket all the way back in Florida. At nine o'clock a Democrat Party official confirmed that a planned fireworks display over the Hudson, a sort of pre-emptive victory celebration, had been cancelled. This came amid rumours that Clinton's hold on key states was slipping, and that a quantity of the celebration fireworks had gone missing in suspicious circumstances. At ten o'clock, Donald Trump left the Republican festivities at the New York Hilton Midtown and retired for the evening to his penthouse apartment atop Trump Tower on Fifth Avenue.

He turned on the television, changed into his pyjamas, brushed and flossed his teeth and climbed into an otherwise empty bed. He watched the news for only a few minutes before turning off both television and bedside lamp. It had been a long, hard day. It had been a long, hard year. A year like this took its toll on a man.

Donald couldn't say how long he had been lying in bed, if he had even fallen asleep at all, when a sudden and stark light filled his bedroom, reflecting off mirrors and gilt-edged surfaces alike. He pushed himself up onto one elbow and held out his hand against the light.

"Who's there?" he said.

The light was held aloft by a tall figure.

"Come here and know me better, man," it said in a deep and self-important voice.

Donald threw the sheets aside and, both fearful and curious, tried to find his slippers with questing bare feet. "That light's a bit bright," he said.

"Some men think so," said the self-important figure. The light dimmed a little anyway, to the point where Donald could see the figure properly.

It stood by the window atop piles of boxes and crates that had not been there before. At first glance it appeared to be an imposing, almost god-like figure, wrapped in ancient senatorial robes, a spiked crown upon its head and a flaming torch held aloft in its right hand. A further inspection might have inferred the robe was nothing but one of Donald's own bedsheets, the crown had been fashioned out of wire coat hangers and the torch was a battery-operated plastic piece of crap that sold for fifteen bucks at the gift shop on Liberty Island. Donald was too stunned to notice.

"I am the Spirit of America," intoned the dread visage.

"The Spirit of...?"

"Of America."

"Wow," said Donald. "Does this mean I've won?"

"What?"

"I assumed that when I won the election, I would have a visit from the CIA or NSA – to tell me the nuclear launch codes or the truth about Area 51 or something. But this— Believe me, this is very impressive."

Clovenhoof faltered. He'd been ready for Trump to cower in fear. He'd been ready for Trump to wallop him one and denounce him as a fraud. He hadn't been ready for Trump to assume a visit from the Statue of Liberty to be standard operating procedure for a newly elected president.

"You think you've won the election?"

Trump gave him a content and unruffled look. "Those poll numbers are looking very good. I know we're already winning bigly in key states."

"You cannot be president," insisted Clovenhoof.

"Ah," said Trump. "I see what's going on. You're one of those Democrat vote riggers."

"The vote is not rigged," said Clovenhoof, wishing he'd thought of that. "No sane American would want you as its commander in chief."

"I am a very, very smart person," said Trump. "I have heard from hundreds of people that tell me how smart I am, believe me. Important people too. I'm not a politician but I am a businessman.

Who will the American people trust to lead them? Hillary is really, really a not good leader."

"Foolish mortal!" Clovenhoof towered over him. "Do you think you are fit to hold the same office as the great George Washington?"

"George Washington who kept slaves on his Virginia plantation?"

"Abraham Lincoln then," snapped Clovenhoof.

"People tell me that Abraham Lincoln censored the press and had his enemies deported. I don't know, but that's what people tell me," said Trump.

"You dare besmirch the name of one this country's great heroes?"

"Hero? He was a hero because he freed some slaves and got shot in a theatre? Personally, I like people who don't get shot in the back of the head."

Clovenhoof, who was not used to trying to take the moral high ground, was finding it exhausting. He flung his Lady Liberty torch aside, jumped down from the crate he was stood on and plumped for a moment of honesty.

"Listen, buddy. You can't be president."

"That's what the GOP bigwigs said. That's what Rubio and Cruz said. People underestimate me."

"But you can't." Clovenhoof thrust his much crumpled Apocalypse Bingo sheet in Trump's face. "Nostradamus' Apocalypse Bingo sheet says that when the Trump of Doom sounds in victory then 'All the countries of the world will end in flame and ordeal.'"

"All the Countries of the World?" said Trump thoughtfully. He snatched the paper and scoured it. "Who concocted this nonsense?"

"Nostradamus, you gibbon."

Trump screwed the paper up and tossed it aside. "I don't buy it. Why would my presidency – and it will be an amazing presidency, just you wait – why would it bring about the end of the world?"

"Seriously? The thought of your little mitts on the big red nuclear button is causing half the world sleepless nights as it is."

Trump frown furiously. "What are you saying?"

"I'm saying—"

"Little mitts? Big red button? Look at these hands. Are these small hands? These fingers. Look at them. Long and beautiful. That button will look positively tiny with my hand on it. Let me tell you, when I push a button, the button knows it's been pushed. I've had no complaints."

"No, that's not the point," said Clovenhoof with a patience he really didn't have. "I wasn't talking about your schlong, Don."

"Who said you were?"

"I'm saying you're a force of chaos. I mean, I don't normally have a problem with that. I generally applaud it. Seriously. Kudos to you. You've spent your life dicking about with other people's money. Build a casino, go bankrupt, build a hotel, go bankrupt. And all those women— I respect your love of good ol' T & A, although the only time you'll find me grabbing anything is at grab-a-granny night at the Boldmere Oak. And you've got that hottie Melanoma as your wife."

"My wife is Melania."

"Twins? Kinky. See! I would normally take my hat off you." Clovenhoof cast off his makeshift crown and frisbeed it into a corner. "You're like me. Living the dream. But we can't have you at the steering wheel of the free world. Saying you're going to build that wall on the Mexican border. Saying you're going to put Hillary in jail. Saying you'll leave NATO, pull out of climate change deals, ban Muslims from the US. Crazy cool ideas, Don, but you can't go through with them. We need a dull prude like Michael in charge while we party on at the back of the bus."

Trump frowned, as though remembering something. He went to his bedside, picked up the television remote and turned the TV back on.

"You hear what I'm saying?" said Clovenhoof.

"Sure," said Trump, disinterestedly. "You don't want me to be President. I hear you. Because you think the world's going to end."

"So, you'll do it?" said Clovenhoof.

"Do it?"

"Make phone calls. Call up Obama. I don't know. Tell them that you're no longer standing."

"Oh, that," said Trump and pulled a face. "No. I'm not doing that. I'm going to be the President."

"I will kill you if you don't step down," warned Clovenhoof, more irritated than threatening.

Trump sat down on the edge of the bed, chuckling as he flicked through the TV channels. "Sure. I don't think I'm going to take a dream threat seriously."

"Dream?" Clovenhoof gave a little shriek of annoyance. "Fine. Screw you, Mr President."

He turned to the massive crates he'd sneakily and improbably hauled into Trump's penthouse bedroom. Irritation gave him strength and nails flew out as he ripped the lid off one. Fat tubes of industrial-sized fireworks sat among polystyrene foam flakes. Clovenhoof pulled out two rockets, each as long as his arm, and sat them on the edge of the crate while he searched for fuse wire.

"And I thought Hillary had cancelled the fireworks because she knew she was going to lose," said Trump. "There!"

"What?" said Clovenhoof.

Trump jiggled his remote at the TV screen. "I knew I had seen it. I have a very, very, very good memory."

On screen was the BBC World News channel. Six individuals were being led away in handcuffs. Nearly all were naked. A huge man was covered in what appeared to be tomato sauce and feathers. A wiry woman fought against her bonds and swore like only an Irishwoman could. An archangel that Clovenhoof knew very well was downcast, a dejected frown and a massive bruise on his face.

"And as the emergency services put out the remaining fires," the newscaster was saying, "the members of All the Countries of the World are all being taken into custody and everyone is glad that this ordeal has come to a satisfactory conclusion. We are sure that in the next few days, commentators will be picking over the precise meaning of the group's surrealist statement. Was it crime or was it art?"

"You see?" said Trump, turning it off. "I am a smart guy. I saw this earlier and this is a dream. I am smarter than you, dream."

"The world's not going to end?" said Clovenhoof. "The prophecy wasn't about the world— It was about—" He sighed. "Nostradamus is a dick."

"So," said Trump, hitching his thumb over his shoulder. "You can leave now. I need my sleep."

Clovenhoof thought on this for a moment. "Um. No," he said, and unspooled a length of fuse across the floor.

"No?" said Trump.

"No." Clovenhoof entwined one end of the fuse wire with that of a rocket, jammed it nose down in the crate then piled a bunch of other fireworks on top of it.

"But the world's not going to end now. You said."

Clovenhoof turned on him. "The world can end in any number of ways, can't it, Don? I've not yet seen the latest series of *Game of Thrones*. With you as President, I'd rate the chances of me having time enough to do that as fifty-fifty at best."

"You talk like Hillary. Do you think I would do a worse job than her?"

Clovenhoof dug in his bedsheet robes for some matches. After a moment he tore the damned thing off and, far more sensibly, dug around in his pockets instead. "I've heard your campaign promises," he said.

Trump laughed at that. He laughed hard.

"I have!" said Clovenhoof. "I've heard them repeated by some of the most monumental morons I could ever meet: your supporters."

Trump pursed his lips, not a disagreement with Clovenhoof's assessment of his supporters, more a disapproval of how it was expressed.

Clovenhoof struck a match. It went out. "You said you would ban Muslims coming into the country."

Trump gave him a reproachful look. "We can't do a blanket ban on a religion, can we?"

"You're going to leave NATO."

"And weaken our own nation's security? I don't think so."

Clovenhoof struck a second match. "What about that wall with Mexico?" The match went out.

"It was a great campaign device. Maybe there'll be a fence. In some places."

"You're going to scrap Obamacare."

"Actually, there are some good aspects that we really, really should keep."

Clovenhoof lit a third match and it caught. "You're going to put Hillary Clinton in jail." He put the match to the end of the fuse. The fuse sparkled as the point of flame moved along it.

"I don't want to hurt the Clintons," said Trump, as though Clovenhoof had just said something patently stupid. "I want to move forward, I don't want to move back."

Clovenhoof just stared at him. In the silence, the fuse hissed its way towards several hundred pounds of explosives.

"If you're not going to do those things, what are you going to do?"

Trump shrugged. "Settle the Trump University lawsuit to get it off my back. Then I need to fill some cabinet posts. My son-in-law Jared will make an excellent White House staffer. I'll find a job for Rudi, get Ben Carson to head up something like education. Scott Pruitt can run the EPA. That'll put the wind up them. Mitt Romney, Newt Gingrich. Oh, and Steve Bannon will make an excellent chief of staff."

"Steve Bannon?"

"The Breitbart guy."

"Ah. Yeah, I've read that website. 'Birth Control makes Women Unattractive and Crazy.'"

"That's one of theirs," said Trump. "Very, very, very insightful."

"But what about the things you promised in your campaign?"

Trump, still convinced he was dreaming, pondered this unhurriedly as the fuse burned away. "There's one promise I've kept."

"Yes?" said Clovenhoof.

"I said I would win."

"But ... but that's— It's underhanded. It's lying. You've cheated and swindled your way to the top. Fine, you're not going to do all the mad and dangerous things you promised. That means you just played on the prejudices of gullible idiots, you used them just so – what? – so you could get the most powerful job in the world and the mansion and jets and honeys that go with it? You've conned a country to line your own pockets and satisfy your own ego and—"

Clovenhoof stopped.

Clovenhoof thought a little.

Clovenhoof scratched his chin.

Clovenhoof went to the crate of fireworks and ripped out the fuse and tossed it away for it to fizz harmlessly in the corner by itself.

"And I just want to shake your hand," he said.

And he did. And Trump did.

"Why?" said Trump.

"You did everything I would do. I would have slipped a few extra fake turds and knob gags in there but, apart from that, you were me to the letter. And you won. You actually won."

"The final results aren't in yet."

"No. You won."

"I said I would," said Trump.

"Well done, Donald."

"Thank you."

Clovenhoof took his phone out and scrolled through for Michael's number.

"And you know what Donald, in another twenty years—" Clovenhoof looked at Trump's waistline "—maybe another ten years, I think there might be a job for you in my old place. They could *use* someone like you." He called Michael. It started to ring.

Trump clicked his fingers and held out his hand. "May I have those matches?"

"Why?"

"Because there's fireworks, dumbass."

Clovenhoof tossed him the book of matches.

The phone went to voicemail.

"Michael. Jeremy. I see your plans went completely tits up. I could have told you that. Anyway, I'm heading home, but I'm going to need you to wire me the money for the flight. That credit card you leant me maxed out, you tight arse."

Trump ambled over to the open crate of fireworks and tucked a huge rocket under his arm. He pushed the balcony window open and tried to juggle the rocket in one arm and the matches in the other.

"And wire it soon. I just don't think I'm needed here anymore."

Trump had the match alight. He grinned as he took aim with the rocket and put the flame to the touch paper.

"America's in very capable hands," said Clovenhoof.

9ᵗʰ November 2016

Sutton Coldfield, Birmingham

Nerys always accepted a cup of tea when Andy offered. Andy and Michael kept in a good stock of high quality biscuits, and that wasn't the sort of thing you turned down.

"So, from what I can understand, this whole thing was one of those misunderstandings," she said through a mouthful of chocolate Hobnob. "Heinz is going to try to play it off as a piece of guerrilla art, a Dadaist statement on the refugee crisis or something. You know the kind of thing."

Andy regarded her levelly. "I don't think I do."

"No, nor me. Well, there's good news and bad news. The good news is that a legal genius by the name of Stefan Grösswang is well on course to getting Michael out of prison. The bad news is that Jeremy's on his way there to act as a character witness."

Andy's face fell. "This is worse than I thought." He pulled out his phone.

"You can't call him now," said Nerys.

"I'm not calling him. I'm ordering some French cheese, German sausage and Italian clothes while I still can," said Andy. "Before Jeremy causes an international incident and has us thrown out of the EU early."

Elsewhere...

Halfway over the Atlantic, Clovenhoof's eight day bout of constipation came to a sudden end with a cacophonous anal fanfare.

He emerged from the aeroplane toilet and declared, "Now, *that's* what I call a trump of doom!"

Such was the stench of ordure and the fear of combustible gases in a confined space that the pilot declared an emergency and the flight was diverted to the Canary Islands.

Clovenhoof left the airport and wandered into a local bar. He looked at the television. To his delight, the news was showing the video of his song *I Kissed a Goat and It Bit Me.* Michael's tomfoolery had at least got his song the recognition it so surely deserved.

There was a microphone and small stage at the rear of the bar. He picked up the microphone and gestured grandly to the smattering of patrons.

"This seems like a nice place. Not as many canaries as I expected, but nice. Bring me alcohol, find me a goat and spread the word. The Trump of Doom will perform his latest hit live. With actions."

Authors' notes

Hello dear reader,

You, we assume, fall into one of two broad categories:

(A) You are a person who is broadly familiar with the real-world events mentioned in this book. Perhaps you lived through them. Perhaps you are living through them right now (poor you). Or you are a future historian and have studied these events in an attempt to understand them (good luck with that!)

(B) You have no knowledge of the events mentioned in this book. Perhaps you are a future person who chose not to study history. Perhaps western civilisation has collapsed and even the concept of 'book' is a fairly novel one. Or perhaps you are living through these strange current times but have not paid any attention to these particular events because you're focussed on something more important, like why your Samsung phone keeps exploding or why the great nations of the world are dropping bombs on your desert home.

Whether you're (A) or (B), this book perhaps needs explaining a little.

Jeremy Clovenhoof is not a political creature. His personal manifesto amounts to 'let it all hang out and party like a drunk divorcee'. The Clovenhoof books are not political books either. Their message, if they have one, is buried under layers of swearing, nudity and the kind of slapstick that even the Three Stooges wouldn't lower themselves to. Seriously, one of Heide's key roles in the editing stage is to delete anything that looks even vaguely intelligent. We're not here to change the world.

However, 2016 has just been one of those years. And we felt we had to write something.

The world is still recovering from a global recession. The rich are getting richer and the poor are getting poorer. Political and military tensions are rising. In such times, people tend to become nostalgic and, on the world stage, the US and Russia seem keen to replay some of their Cold War favourites. In such times, people become frightened. They cling to old prejudices, they reject what they don't understand. They listen to charlatans and mountebanks (Heide will later delete this word for being vaguely intelligent and replace it with the word 'cockwombles'). Recent votes in the UK and the US seem to indicate a rejection of the entire establishment. Upcoming elections in mainland Europe are promising to do the same. All bets are off. These are the 'interesting times' that the Chinese cursed us with.

Anyway, that's why we wrote this book. It goes without saying that most of it is stupid, derivative and, above all else, A WORK OF FICTION. We have not consulted any of the real life characters who we have used or referenced in this piece. We have not written it with their blessing. Any misrepresentation of these individuals is either accidental or done purely for comedic purposes.

That said, it is based on some real events and, as always, some of the things you probably don't think are true are true and vice versa. So, just to set the record straight...

YES – The Toblerone bar was changed shape so there was a lot less 'mountain' and a lot more 'valley'. British people were genuinely upset by this.
NO – Nostradamus didn't write any of the prophecies in this book.
YES – Topless Darts on Ice was a real television programme.
NO – It's not coming back.
YES – In the Rio Olympics, the diving pool turned bright green and no one could explain why.
YES – The European Space Agency's Schiaparelli Mars lander crashed into the Red Planet on 19th October.
YES – The Finnish Eurovision Song Contest entry for 1982 was Kojo with the song, 'Nuku Pommiin'. It scored no points. You can watch it on YouTube if you like.

NO – That guy hitting the big drum is not Heinz Takala.

YES – Ireland did win Eurovision three times in a row. This was arguably an artistic success and a financial disaster.

NO – Aisling McQuillan did not write any of those winning hits.

YES – The electors in the US electoral college system (the people who actually cast the state's votes) can choose to ignore the public vote and pledge their state's votes for the other candidate. People who do this are called 'faithless electors'. Doing this is perfectly legal in 21 states and it does happen.

YES – A vote cast in Wyoming is worth three times as much as a vote cast in New York.

YES – Joseph Smith, founder of the Mormons, believed that Eden was in Missouri and that God lives on a star called Kolob.

YES – On 9th December, Fox News identified Nigel Farage as the British opposition leader.

NO – Nigel Farage is not the official leader of the opposition. He is not a member of the UK parliament, is not the leader of a UK political party and has no official role within UK politics.

YES – Donald Trump has said that the issue of "7-Eleven" is close to his heart. He probably meant 9/11

YES – On 9/11, Trump spoke to a New York television station and pointed out that, with the collapse of the World Trade Centre, Trump Tower was now the tallest building in Manhattan.

NO – The US secret service can detect elephants.

YES – Mike Pence's secret service codename is Hoosier.

NO – JFK's secret service codename was not Hooters.

YES – It was alleged by a former friend and former Conservative party donor that former British Prime Minister, David Cameron, put his penis in a dead pig's mouth.

NO – There is absolutely no evidence to corroborate this allegation.

YES – All the silly EU laws Michael mentions on the road to Romania have appeared in UK newspapers.

NO – None of them are true. All of them are made up. By British newspapers, not us.

YES – Romania was disqualified from entering the 2016 Eurovision Song Contest.

NO – It wasn't because they stole the Lucky Eurovision Gibson SG. There's no such thing.

YES – The bucium is a real instrument and as described.

YES – There are liqueurs, made by monks, which are believed to bestow life-giving properties. Amaro del Capo consists of herbs, flowers, fruit and roots from the Calabrian region of Italy infused in the finest alcohol to aid digestion and give a feeling of wellbeing.

YES – Some Americans believe Hillary has a double who attends functions on her behalf.

YES – Some Americans believe Hillary is in a lesbian relationship with Huma Abedin.

YES – Some Americans believe the missing e-mails kept on Hillary's private server implicate her in a number of state-sanctioned assassinations.

YES – Some Americans believe a Democrat-focussed conspiracy killed Vince Foster, Ron Brown and Kathleen Willey's cat.

YES – Some Americans believe that 'chemtrails', the fictional chemical sprayed from the wingtips of jumbo jets, are killing off the angels in heaven.

YES - Re-read those last five statements. Now go google them. Seriously.

YES – In Mondsee, you can visit the church where Maria is married in *The Sound of Music*. Tour buses visit it on a daily basis.

YES - Under the Austrian anti-Nazi Prohibition Act, you can be arrested and jailed for giving a Nazi salute or shouting 'Heil Hitler'.

YES – Trump accused the Democrats of paying people $1,500 to disrupt Trump rallies.

YES – Trump made many allegations that the Democrats were rigging the election.

YES – Following a shout of 'Gun!', Trump was rushed from the stage of his Reno rally on 5th November.

NO – There was no gun. There was a man called Austyn Crites, a Republican, who had brought a 'Republicans against Trump' sign with him. He was arrested but released without charge.

YES – The 27km long Large Hadron Collider, operated by CERN, runs under both Switzerland and France.

NO – It's probably not possible to drive from Reno to Florida in the time that Clovenhoof manages it in. With no sleep and a loose attitude to speed limits, it'd be close but no.

YES – Allegedly, Margaret Thatcher banned the BBC from playing the *Havana Let's Go* song *Torpedoes* for fear of causing upset during the Falklands Conflict.

YES – An Asian elephant did make a surprising appearance at a Trump rally in Sarasota, Florida. However, that was in April 2016, not November.

NO – Chickens and doves are not the same animal and no EU directive says they are.

NO – The Large Hadron Collider cannot make a black hole, accidentally or deliberately. Some people believe it can but they're not scientists.

YES – Up until Clovenhoof's conversation with him in New York, every piece of dialogue attributed to Donald Trump in this book was a direct quote as reported by US or UK media and given in the situation portrayed.

NO – Clovenhoof and Donald Trump did not meet on the night of the election, obviously. Donald Trump is not known to have said any of the things he said in that conversation. It's fiction, folks.

YES – However, in that conversation, all those things Trump said he would do, starting with settling the Trump University lawsuit and finishing with the appointment of Steve Bannon to his staff are things he has done or tried to do since becoming President-elect.

YES – Steve Bannon's Breitbart News publishes news stories with headlines like, 'Birth control makes woman unattractive and crazy.'

YES – Trump appointed Scott Pruitt to run the Environment Protection Agency. Pruitt does not believe that manmade climate change exists.

YES – Trump has spoken publicly more than once about the size and beauty of his fingers/penis.

YES – The Democrats did cancel their New York fireworks display on election night.

NO – Clovenhoof didn't steal them.

YES – Donald Trump won the election. What are you going to do about it?

Thanks, Mike!

A conversation, paraphrased.

"Hey, Mike."
"Sup?"
"You know that great job you do for us on our books?"
"I sure do. I'm a professional and always do a great job and am rightly rewarded for my efforts with actual money and none of that 'exposure' nonsense."
"Well, we've decided to write a novella about Trump but we've only got a month to do it in. Stupid, huh?"
"The novella's stupid? Or Trump? Or the fact that you've only given yourself a month to write a 40,000 word book?"
"We couldn't really say. Anyway, that brilliant thing you do for us, that usually takes five weeks. Can you do it in five days?"
"I sure can."
"Wow! You're amazing, Mike. Thanks!"

(Mike Chinn is an amazing editor. Mike Watts is an amazing illustrator. Both are googleable.)

About the Authors

Heide and Iain are currently citizens of the European Union, although possibly not for much longer.
They are married but not to each other.

Heide lives in North Warwickshire with her husband and children.
Iain lives in south Birmingham with his wife and daughters.

19532007R00092

Printed in Great Britain
by Amazon